"What Will It Be?" Tennessee Asked. "September Canyon, Or Back To The Ranch House?"

Diana looked at him. Part of her was frankly terrified at the prospect of being alone with him for days on end. Part of her was not—and in some ways that was most terrifying of all.

Shutting out everything, she closed her eyes. *What am I going to do?*

The image of Tennessee's powerful hands holding a kitten with such care condensed in her mind. *I never knew a man could be so gentle with anything.*

The ingrained habit of years made her mind veer away from the bleak night when she had learned once and forever to distrust men, and her own judgment.

Unbidden came a thought that made her tremble with a tangle of emotions she refused to name and a question she knew she shouldn't ask, even in the silence of her own mind.

Would Tennessee be as gentle with a woman as he was with that kitten?

Dear Reader,

Welcome to Silhouette Desire! Naturally, I think you've made a spectacular choice because, for me, each and every Silhouette Desire novel is a delightful, romantic, unique book. And once you start reading your selection I *know* you'll agree!

Silhouette Desire is thrilling romance. Here you'll encounter the joys and even some of the tribulations of falling in love. You'll meet characters you'll get to know and like . . . and heroes you'll get to know and *love*. Sensuous, moving, compelling, these are all words you can use to describe Silhouette Desire. But remember, words are not enough—you must *read* and get the total experience!

And there is something wonderful in store for you this month: *Outlaw*, the first in Elizabeth Lowell's WESTERN LOVERS series. It tells the story of rough-and-tough Tennesee Blackthorne . . . a man of fiery passions and deep emotions.

Of course, *all* of February's Silhouette Desire books are terrific—don't miss a single one! Until next month . . .

All the best,

Lucia Macro
Senior Editor

ELIZABETH LOWELL

OUTLAW

SILHOUETTE *Desire*®

Published by Silhouette Books New York

America's Publisher of Contemporary Romance

SILHOUETTE BOOKS
300 East 42nd St., New York, N.Y. 10017

OUTLAW

ISBN: 0-373-05624-9

First Silhouette Books printing February 1991

Printed in the U.S.A.

Books by Elizabeth Lowell

Silhouette Desire

Summer Thunder #77
The Fire of Spring #265
Too Hot to Handle #319
Love Song for a Raven #355
Fever #415
Dark Fire #462
Fire and Rain #546
Outlaw #624

Silhouette Intimate Moments

The Danvers Touch #18
Lover in the Rough #34
Summer Games #57
Forget Me Not #72
A Woman Without Lies #81
Traveling Man #97
Valley of the Sun #109
Sequel #128
Fires of Eden #141
Sweet Wind, Wild Wind #178
Chain Lightning #256

ELIZABETH LOWELL

is a pseudonym for Ann Maxwell, who also writes with her husband under the name of A.E. Maxwell. Her novels range from science fiction to historical fiction, and from romance to the sometimes gritty reality of modern suspense. All of her novels share a common theme—the power and beauty of love.

For Isabel Swift,
who permits a variety of romance stories

One

Diana Saxton drove into the Rocking M's dusty ranch yard and shut off the car's engine. The first thing she saw was a cowboy as big as a barn door standing on the front porch. Unconsciously her hands clenched on the wheel, betraying her instant unease in the presence of men in general and big, well-built men in particular.

The ranch house's front door opened and closed. When another equally big, hard-looking man in boots and jeans came out of the house and began walking toward Diana, carrying a geologist's hammer. Over toward the corral, a third cowboy was climbing onto a horse. The man was so big that he made the horse look like a kid's pony.

My God, Diana thought, *don't they have any normal-size men out here?* Crowding that thought came another. *I can't spend a summer close to these men! But then, I won't have to. I'll be at the September Canyon site.*

Someone called out from the house. Diana recognized Carla MacKenzie's voice and let out a soundless sigh of relief as the first big man turned immediately and went back inside at the sound of his name. Luke MacKenzie, Carla's husband.

As a bit of Diana's uneasiness faded, she recognized the second man. Cash McQueen, Carla's half brother. He was coming toward Diana, slipping the hammer into a loop on his leather belt as he walked. Hastily she got out of her car. She had learned in the past few years not to show her distrust of men—especially big men—yet she still couldn't force herself to be close to any man in a confined space, particularly a car.

Before Cash got to Diana, another call from the house stopped him. He waved to her, said something she couldn't understand and went back into the ranch house.

A sudden burst of activity outside the corral caught Diana's attention. A horse had its head down between its forelegs, its back was steeply arched and its body was uncoiling like a released spring. A few spectacular bucks later, the horse's beefy rider lost his grip on the saddle. He hit the ground, rolled to his hands and knees and came up onto his feet with a lunge. He grabbed the bridle close to the bit and began beating the horse with a heavy quirt. The horse screamed and tried to escape but was helpless against the cruel grip on the bridle.

Without stopping to think, Diana started toward the terrified horse, yelling at the man to stop. Before she had taken three steps, a man in a light blue shirt vaulted the corral fence and landed like a cat, running toward the brutal cowboy, gaining speed with every stride. The running man was smaller and unarmed, hardly a fair match against the huge, beefy man wielding a whip.

Behind Diana, the ranch house door slammed and men came running. Another man ran out of the barn, saw what was happening and yelled, "Careful, ramrod! Baker's quirt has lead shot in it!"

Baker wheeled to face Tennessee Blackthorn, the Rocking M's ramrod. Baker flipped the quirt over in his hand, wielding the thick leather stock as a club rather than using the whip end against Ten. When his thick arm lifted, Diana screamed and men shouted. Only Ten was silent. He closed the last few feet between himself and Baker as the lead-weighted quirt came smashing down.

Ten didn't flail with his fists or duck away from the blow. The edge of his left hand connected with Baker's wrist. The quirt went spinning up and away, flying end over end through the air. Simultaneously the ramrod's right fist delivered a short, chopping blow to Baker's heart. Ten pivoted, slammed an elbow into Baker's diaphragm and sent another chopping blow to his neck as the big man bent over, folding up, all fight gone. Before the quirt even hit the ground, Baker was stretched out full length facedown in the dirt, unmoving.

Torn between disbelief and shock, Diana came to a stop, staring at the Rocking M's ramrod. She shook her head, trying to understand how a man who was six inches shorter and sixty pounds lighter than his adversary had begun and ended a fight before the bigger man could land a blow. As though at a distance she heard Cash and Luke go by her, moving more slowly now.

"Nice work, Ten," Luke said.

"Amen," said Cash. Then, to Luke, "Remind me never to pick a fight with your ramrod. Somebody taught that boy how to play hardball."

Ten said nothing, for he was more interested in calming the frightened horse than in talking about the brief fight. "Easy, girl. Easy now. No one's going to hurt you. Easy...easy."

As he spoke, he approached the sweating, trembling mare. When he saw streaks of blood mixed with the horse's lather, he swore, but the soothing tone of his voice never changed despite the scalding nature of his words. Slowly he closed his hands around the reins and began checking over the mare.

As Ten's hands moved over the animal, it began to calm down. Not once did the ramrod look toward the motionless Baker. Ten knew precisely how much damage he had done to the brutal cowboy; what Ten wanted to know was how badly the horse had been hurt.

Cash sat on his heels next to Baker and checked for a visible injuries. There was nothing obvious. After a few moments Cash stood and said, "Out cold, but still breathing."

Luke grunted. "Any permanent damage?"

"Not that I can see."

"He won't be swinging a quirt for a while," Ten said without looking up from the mare. "Not with his right hand, anyway. I broke his wrist."

"Too bad it wasn't his neck," Luke said. "You warned him last week about beating a horse." Luke turned to Cosy, who had yelled the warning about the quirt to Ten. "Bring the truck around. You're on garbage detail tonight."

"Where to?" asked Cosy.

"West Fork."

"Forty miles out and forty miles back, damn near all of it on dirt roads," Cosy grumbled. "In the old days we'd have dumped his carcass on the ranch boundary and let him walk to town."

"Not on the Rocking M," Luke said, stretching lazily. "My great-granddaddy Case MacKenzie once killed a man for beating a horse."

Slowly Diana retreated, walking backward for a few steps before turning and moving quickly toward her car. Though she was a student of human history—Anasazi history, to be precise—she wasn't accustomed to having her history lessons served to her raw. She didn't like having it pointed out that the veneer of civilization was quite thin, even in modern times, and it was especially thin in men.

I shouldn't be shocked. I know better than most women what men are like underneath their shirts and ties, shaving lotions and smiles. Savages and outlaws. All of them. Outlaws who use their strength against those who are weaker.

A vivid picture came to Diana's mind—the man called Ten coming over the fence, attacking the big cowboy, reducing the larger man to unconsciousness with a few violent blows. She shuddered.

"Diana? What happened?"

She looked up and saw Carla standing on the front porch, holding a tiny baby in her arms.

"One of the men was beating a horse," Diana said.

"Baker." Carla's mouth flattened from its usual generous curve. "Ten warned him."

"He did more than that. He beat him unconscious."

"Ten? That doesn't sound like him. I've never seen him lose his temper."

"Is he your ramrod?"

Carla nodded. "Yes, he's the Rocking M's foreman."

"Light blue shirt, black hair, small?"

"Small?" she asked, surprised. "I don't think of Ten as small."

"He's a lot smaller than Baker."

"Oh, well, even Luke and Cash are smaller than Baker. But Ten's at least six feet tall. A bit more, I think." Carla stood on tiptoe and looked out toward the corral. "Is he all right?"

"His wrist is broken."

"Ten's hurt? Oh my God, I've got to—"

"Not Ten," Diana interrupted quickly. "Baker is the one with a broken wrist."

"Oh." Relief changed Carla's face from strained to pretty. "Then Ten will take care of it. He's had medic training." She looked closely at Diana. "You're pale. Are you all right?"

Diana closed her eyes. "I'm fine. It was a long drive out and the road was rough. Now I know why. I was going back in time as well as miles."

Laughing, shaking her head, Carla shifted the sleeping baby and held out her hand to Diana. "Come in and have some coffee. French roast, Colombian beans, with just enough Java beans blended in to give the coffee finesse as well as strength.''

Diana's eyelids snapped open. The dark blue of her eyes was vivid against her still-pale face. "I'm hallucinating. They didn't have French roast in the Old West, did they?''

"I don't know, but this isn't the Old West.''

"You could have fooled me,'' Diana said, thinking about outlaws and brawls and a man with the lethal quickness of a cat. But despite her thoughts, she allowed Carla to lead her across the porch and into the cool ranch house. "Your ramrod would have made one hell of an outlaw.''

"In the old days, a lot of good men were outlaws. They had no choice. There wasn't any law to be *in*side of.'' Carla laughed at the expression on Diana's face. "But don't worry. The bad old days are gone. Look in our side yard. There's a satellite dish out there sucking up all kinds of ex-otic signals from space. We have television, a VCR, radios, CD players, personal computers, a dishwasher, microwave, washer-dryer—the whole tortilla.''

"And cowboys swinging quirts full of lead shot,'' Diana muttered.

"Is that what Baker did?''

Diana nodded.

"My God. No wonder Ten lost his temper.''

"What temper? He looked about as angry as a man chopping wood.''

Carla shook her head unhappily. "Poor Ten. He's had a tough time ramrodding this crew in the past year.''

" 'Poor Ten' looked like he could handle it,'' Diana said beneath her breath.

"The ranch is so remote it's hard to get good men to stay. I don't know how we'd manage without Ten. And now that we've found museum-quality Anasazi artifacts in September Canyon, the pothunters are descending in hordes. Someone has to stay at the site all the time. Cash has been doing it, but he has to leave tomorrow for the Andes. We're going to be more shorthanded than ever.''

"The Andes, huh? Great. Everybody deserves a vacation," Diana said, cheered by the thought that there would be one less big man on the Rocking M.

"Cash isn't exactly going on a vacation. One of his colleagues thinks there's a mother lode back up on the flanks of one of those nameless granite peaks. That's the one thing Cash can't resist."

"Nameless peaks?"

"Hard rock and gold. Ten calls Cash the Granite Man but swears it's because of Cash's hard head, not his love of hard-rock mining."

Carla tucked the baby into an old-fashioned cradle that was next to the kitchen table. The baby stirred, opened sleepy turquoise eyes and slid back into sleep once more as Carla slowly rocked the cradle.

"How's the little man doing?" Diana asked softly, bending over the baby until her short, golden brown hair blended with the honey finish of the cradle.

"Growing like a weed in the sun. Logan's going to be at least as big as his daddy."

Diana looked at the soft-cheeked, six-week-old baby and tried to imagine it fully grown, as big as Luke, beard stubbled and powerful. "You'd better start domesticating this little outlaw real soon or you'll never have a chance."

Carla laughed in the instant before she realized that Diana was serious. She looked at the older woman for a moment, remembering the class she had taken from Dr. Diana Saxton, artist and archaeologist, a woman who was reputed not to think much of men. At the time Carla had dismissed the comments as gossip; now she wasn't sure.

"You make it sound like I'm going to need a whip and a chair," Carla said.

"Those are the customary tools for dealing with wild animals, and men are definitely in that category. What a pity that it takes one to make a baby."

"Not all men are like Baker."

Diana made a sound that could have been agreement or disbelief as she began stroking the baby's cheek with a gentle fingertip, careful not to awaken him. She admired the perfect, tiny eyelashes, the snub nose, the flushed lips, the miniature fingers curled in relaxation on the pale cradle blanket. Gradually she noticed more of the cradle itself, how the grain of the wood had been perfectly matched to the curves of the cradle, how the pieces had been fitted without nails, how the wood itself had been polished to a gentle satin luster.

"What a beautiful cradle," Diana said softly, running her fingertips over the wood. "It's a work of art. Where did you get it?"

"Luke made it. He has wonderful hands, strong and gentle."

Diana looked at the cradle once more and the baby lying securely within. She tried not to think how much she would like to have a child of her own. Sex was a necessary step toward conception. For sex, a woman had to trust a man not to hurt her—a man who was bigger, stronger and basically more savage than a woman. Years ago, Diana had abandoned the idea of sex. The thought of a baby, however, still haunted her.

"If Luke is gentle with you and little Logan," Diana said quietly, touching the pale blanket with her fingertips, "you're a lucky woman. You have one man in a million."

Before Carla could say anything more, Diana stood and turned away from the cradle.

"I think I'll take a rain check on that coffee. I want to get my stuff unloaded before dinner."

"Of course. We're putting you in the old ranch house where all the artifacts from the site are being kept. Just follow the road out beyond the barn. When the road forks, go to the right. The old house is only about a hundred yards from the barn. Dinner is at six. Don't bother to knock. Just come in the back way. The dining room is just off the kitchen and both rooms have outside doors. We all eat together during the week. Sundays the hands fend for themselves. You'll eat with us.''

Diana looked at the long, narrow room just off the kitchen. Two rectangular tables pushed together all but filled the room. She tried to imagine what it would be like to eat surrounded by big male bodies. The thought was daunting. She took a slow breath, told herself that she would be spending nearly all of her time at the site in September Canyon, and turned back to Carla.

"Thanks," Diana said. "I'll be back at six, whip in one hand and chair in the other."

Two

The alarm on Diana's digital watch cheeped annoyingly, breaking her concentration. She set aside the stack of numbered site photos, reset her watch for a short time later, stretched and heard her stomach rumble in anticipation of dinner. Despite her hunger, she was reluctant to leave the hushed solitude of the old house and the silent companionship of the ancient artifacts lining the shelves of the workroom.

Slanting yellow light came through the north window, deepening the textures of stone and sandal fragments, potshards and glue pots, making everything appear to be infused with a mystic glow. Diana couldn't wait until tomorrow, when she would drive to September Canyon. Photos, artifacts and essays, no matter how precise and scholarly, couldn't convey the complexity of the interlocking mystery of the Anasazi, the land and time.

Her mind more on the past than the present, Diana walked slowly into the bathroom. The slanting light coming through the small, high window made the gold in her hair incandescent and gave the darker strands a rich satin luster. Her eyes became indigo in shadow, vivid sapphire in direct light. The natural pink in her smooth cheeks and lips contrasted with the dark brown of her eyebrows and the dense fringe of her eyelashes.

Once Diana would have noticed her own understated beauty and heightened it with mascara and blusher, lipstick and haunting perfumes. Once, but no longer. Never again would she be accused by a man of using snares and lures to attract members of the opposite sex, then teasing and maddening them with what she had no intention of giving. Never again would she put herself in a position where a man felt entitled to take what he wanted in the belief that it had been offered—and if it hadn't, it should have been.

Soap, water, unscented lotion and a few strokes with a hairbrush through her short, gamine hairstyle and Diana was ready for dinner. She thought longingly of the four-inch heels she wore when she was teaching to add to her own five feet three inches of frankly curved female body, but wearing a cotton pullover sweater big enough for a man and faded jeans with four-inch heels would be ludicrous. Besides, the scarred, rough-country hiking boots she wore most of the time added at least two inches to her height.

And she was going to need every inch of confidence she could get.

"Mmmrreooow."

Diana's head snapped toward the window at the unexpected sound. A lean, tiger-striped cat with one chewed ear was standing outside on the tree limb that brushed against the bathroom window. The cat's forepaw was batting hopefully at the bottom of the window, which was open a crack.

"Hello," Diana said, smiling. "Do you live here?"

The paw, claws politely sheathed, patted again beneath the length of the opening.

"I get the message."

She pushed up the window enough for the cat to come in. It leaped from windowsill to the edge of the sink with an effortless grace that reminded her of the Rocking M's ramrod vaulting the corral fence and landing running.

The cat sniffed Diana's meager toiletries, nosed the peppermint toothpaste, sneezed, *yeowed* softly and stropped itself against her midriff. She ran her palm down the cat's spine, enjoying the supple arch of the animal's body as it rubbed against her in turn. Soon the vibrations of an uninhibited purr were rippling from the cat.

"You're a sweetheart," Diana said. "Would you let me hold you?"

The cat would. In fact, it insisted.

"Goodness, you're heavy! Not fat, though. You must be all muscle."

The purring redoubled.

Laughing softly, Diana smoothed her cheeks and chin against the vibrant bundle of fur. The cat moved sinuously in return, twisting against her in slow motion, relishing the physical contact. And shedding, of course.

Diana looked at the gray and black hairs sticking to the navy cotton sweater she was wearing. She shrugged. Maybe some of the men would be allergic to cats. The thought had a definite appeal.

"C'mon, cat. Let's see if they allow felines in the dining room."

The cat burrowed more tightly into Diana's arms, clinging with just a hint of claws while she closed the bathroom window. Cradling the purring animal, Diana made a quick circuit of the old house, making sure that everything was buttoned up in case the thunderstorm that had been threatening for the past hour actually got down to work. The bedroom was in order—windows shut, clothes put away, sheet turned down on the double bed with its antique headboard and blessedly new mattress set. The window over the kitchen sink was closed. The workroom with its two long tables and countless bins and cubbyholes and shelves was as orderly as it was ever likely to be.

Absently Diana ran her fingertips over the smooth surface of a cabinet, wondering if Luke had made this furniture as well as the cradle. She suspected he had. There was a quality of craftsmanship and care that was rare in modern furniture.

Her stomach growled. She eased her wrist out from under the cat and looked at her watch. Twenty minutes to six. Her alarm would be going off again soon, telling her she had to be where she very much didn't want to be—in a room full of strange men.

Maybe if I get there early, I can grab a plate of food and a seat at the corner of the table. That way I won't be completely surrounded by savages.

Men, not savages, she reminded herself automatically, trying to be fair.

The part of herself that didn't care about fair shot back: *Men or savages. Same difference.*

Diana remembered the fine-grained, carefully wrought cradle and mentally placed a question mark beside Luke's name. It was just possible that he wasn't a savage or an outlaw beyond the pale of gentle society. For Carla's sake, Diana hoped so. Carla had been one of her favorite students—bright, quick, eager, fascinated by the Anasazi's complex, enigmatic past.

The watch alarm cheeped again. The cat's tail whipped in annoyance.

"I agree, cat, but it's the only way I remember to be anywhere. Once I start working over potshards or sketchbooks, everything else just goes away."

The cat made a disgruntled sound and resettled itself more comfortably in her arms.

Diana shut the front door and looked down the narrow path that led from the old ranch house to the bigger, more modern one. Reluctant to confront the Rocking M's oversize men, she lingered for a moment on the front step of the

old house. The grove of dark evergreens that surrounded the
original ranch house was alive with rain-scented wind.
Clouds were seething overhead, their billows set off by
spears of brassy gold light that made the wild bowl of the
sky appear to be supported by shafts of pure light. Distant
thunder rumbled, telling tales of invisible lightning.

She took a deep breath and felt excitement uncurl along
her nerves as the taste of the storm wind swept through her.
She had been cooped up in classrooms too long, earning
money so that she could explore the Anasazi homeland
during the long summer break. The boundless, ancient land
of the Four Corners called to her, singing of people and
cultures long vanished, mysteries whispering among
shadow, shattered artifacts waiting to be made whole. That
was what she had come to the Rocking M for—the undis-
covered past.

Caressing the cat absently with her chin, Diana walked the
short distance to the big house. When the wind shifted, the
smell of food beckoned to her, making her aware of the fact
that she had missed lunch.

The outside door into the dining room was open. Diana
looked in, but nobody was inside yet. From the bunkhouse
beyond the corral came the sound of men calling to one another, talking about the day's work or the pending storm or
the savory smell of dinner on the wind. Quietly Diana
walked the length of the dining room toward the door leading into the kitchen. She had just begun to hope that she
would be able to grab a plate and eat alone when she stepped
into the kitchen and stopped as though her feet had been
nailed to the floor.

There was a man standing with his back to her, a stranger
with wide shoulders stretching against the black fabric of his
shirt. The suggestion of male power was emphasized by the
line of his back tapering down to lean hips, the muscular
ease of his stance and the utter confidence of his posture as
he stood motionless in black jeans and black boots that were
polished by use.

My God, he's as tall and straight and hard as a stone cliff. No wonder he's confident. All he has to do is stand there and he dominates everything.

Reflexively Diana backed up but succeeded only in giving away her presence by bumping into a counter.

"Carla?" the man said, turning around slowly. His voice was deep, slightly rough, a ragged kind of velvet that was as dark as his clothes. His head was bent over something he was holding. His hair was intensely black, subtly curly, thick. "Can you give me a hand?"

Diana opened her mouth to say that she wasn't Carla but was so surprised by what she saw that no words came out.

A tiger-striped kitten lay cupped in the man's lean, callused hands. The contrast between the man's strength and the kitten's soft body was as shocking as the clarity of the man's ice-gray eyes looking at her. Abruptly she realized that she had seen him once before, under very different circumstances.

"Y-you're the ramrod," she said without thinking.

"Most people call me Ten. Short for Tennessee."

"You—Baker—the horse—"

Ten looked more closely at the woman who stood before him, her unease as badly concealed as the alluring curves of her body beneath her loose cotton sweater.

"Don't worry," Ten said. "He won't be back. Have you seen Carla?"

Diana shook her head, making light twist through her short, silky hair. Ten's nostrils flared slightly as he smelled the freshness of soap and sunshine and female skin.

"Think you could put Pounce down long enough to help me with Nosy?"

"Pounce?" Diana asked, wondering if she had lost her mind.

"That sly renegade who's grinning and purring in your arms."

"Oh . . . the cat." Diana looked down. "Pounce, huh?"

Ten made a sound of agreement that was suspiciously like a purr. "Best mouser on the Rocking M. Usually he's standoffish, but he can sense a particular kind of soft touch three miles away. From the smug look on his face, he was right about you."

The kitten stirred as though it wanted to be free. Long fingers closed gently, restraining the tiny animal without hurting or frightening it.

"Easy there, Nosy. That wound has to be cleaned up or you're going to be dead or three-legged, which amounts to the same thing out here. And that would be a shame. You're the best-looking kitten that ugly old mouser has sired."

Bemused by the picture man and kitten made, Diana opened her arms. Pounce took the hint, leaped gracefully to the floor and vanished into the house. Drawn against her will by the kitten's need, Diana bent over Ten's hands.

"What's wrong with it?" she asked.

"She was just living up to her name. Nosy. Either one of the chickens pecked her, or a hawk made a pass at her and she got free, or one of the bunkhouse dogs bit her, or..." Ten shrugged. "Lots of things can happen to a newly weaned kitten on a ranch."

"Poor little thing," Diana murmured, stroking the kitten with a fingertip, noticing for the first time that the fur on the animal's left haunch was rucked up over a knot of swollen flesh. "What do you want me to do?"

"Hold her while I clean her up. Normally her mother would take care of it, but she went hunting a week ago and didn't come back."

Diana looked up for an instant and received a vivid impression of diamond-clear eyes framed by thick black eyelashes that any woman would have envied. The eyelashes were the only suggestion of softness about Ten, but it reassured Diana in an odd way.

"Show me what to do."

The left corner of Ten's mouth tipped upward approvingly. "Hold your hands out. That's it. Now hold Nosy here, and here, so I can get to the haunch. Hold on a little harder. You won't hurt her. She's still at the age where she's all rubber bands and curiosity.''

The description made Diana smile at the same instant that warm, hard fingers pressed over her own, showing her how much restraint to use on the kitten.

"That's good. Now hold tight."

In the silence that came while Ten gently examined the kitten, Diana could hear her own heartbeat and feel the subtle warmth of Ten's breath as he bent over the furry scrap of life she held in her hands.

"Damn. I was afraid of that."

"What?" she asked.

"I'll have to open it up."

Ten reached toward the counter with a long arm. For the first time Diana noticed the open first aid kit. The sound of the wrapper being removed from the sterile, disposable scalpel seemed as loud to her as thunder.

Gray eyes assessed Diana, missing nothing of her distress.

"I'll get Carla," he said.

"No," Diana said quickly. "I'm not squeamish. Well, not horribly squeamish. Everyone who works at remote sites has to go through first aid training. It's just . . . the kitten is so small."

"Close your eyes. It will make it easier on all of us."

Diana closed her eyes and held her breath, expecting to hear a cry of distress from the kitten when Ten went to work. Other than a slight twitch, the animal showed no reaction. Diana was equally still, so still that she sensed the tiny currents of air made when Ten's hands moved over the small patient. The words he spoke to Nosy were like the purring of a mama cat, sound without meaning except the most basic meaning of all—reassurance.

There was the sharp smell of disinfectant, the thin rasp of paper wrappings being torn away and a sense of light pressure as Ten swabbed the wound clean.

"Okay. You can open your eyes now."

Diana looked down. The kitten's haunch was wet, marred only by a tiny cut. Most of the swelling was gone, removed when Ten lanced the boil that had formed over the wound.

"Thorn," Ten said, holding up a wicked, vaguely curved fragment. "Wild rose from the looks of it."

"Will Nosy be all right now?"

"Should be."

Long fingers slid beneath the kitten, moving over Diana's skin almost caressingly as Ten lifted the animal from her hands. Her breath froze, but Ten never so much as glanced at her.

"C'mon, Nosy," he said, cradling the kitten against his neck with his left hand. "You've taken up enough of the lady's time. What you need now is a little sleep and TLC."

"TLC? Is that a medicine?"

The corner of Ten's mouth curved up again. "Best one in the world. Tender Loving Care."

As he spoke, Ten stroked Nosy's face with a fingertip that was as gentle as a whisper. After a few strokes the kitten looked bemused and altogether content. Within moments Nosy's eyelids lowered over round amber eyes. There was a little yawn, the delicate curl of a tiny pink tongue, and the kitten was asleep.

With a feeling of unreality, Diana looked at the ramrod's hard hand curled protectively around the sleeping kitten and remembered that same hand breaking a man's wrist and then slamming him into unconsciousness before he could even cry out in pain.

Ramrod. The name suits him.

But so did the sleeping kitten.

Three

Dinner was on the table at six o'clock, straight up. By long-standing custom, no one waited for latecomers. That included Luke, who was still on the phone talking to the sheriff. No one took Luke's place at the head of the table, but formality ended there. Cash and Carla sat facing Diana and Ten across the table. Diana had managed to secure a seat just to the left of the head of the table, ensuring that she would have only one person seated next to her. Even so, she felt crowded, because that one person was Ten.

To Diana's eyes, the long dining table was supporting enough food for at least twenty people. Five cowhands sat at the other end of the table. There was room for five more men and seven men in a squeeze, but the Rocking M was shorthanded. Only nine people were seated at the moment. Then the outside door banged and a new cowhand called Jervis rushed in and snagged the platter of pork chops before he had even sat down.

"Where's Cosy?" Jervis asked as he slid into a chair and began forking pork chops onto his plate.

"Garbage run," Ten said.

Jervis hesitated, looked around the table and said to Ten, "Baker, huh?"

Ten grunted.

"Who gave him the good word?"

"I did."

"How'd he take it?"

"I didn't hear any complaints."

Cash half strangled on laughter and coffee.

"Something funny?" asked Jervis.

"Ten had Baker laid out cold in six seconds flat," Cash said casually, reaching for the gravy. "He's probably still wondering what hit him."

"Can't say as I'm sorry," Jervis said. He dished a mountain of potatoes onto his plate before he turned and looked Ten over. "Not a mark on you. You must be as much an outlaw as Cosy said you were. That Baker did a lot of bragging about what a fighter he was. Talked about men he'd busted up so bad they pi—er, passed blood for months."

Ten glanced at Diana before he gave the cowhand an icy look. "Jervis, why don't you just shovel food and leave the dinner conversation to Carla. Miss Saxton isn't used to anything less polished than a faculty tea."

"Sorry, ma'am," Jervis said to Diana.

"Don't apologize on my account," she quickly. "Life at remote archaeological sites isn't as polished as Mr., er—"

"Blackthorn," Ten said politely.

"—Blackthorn seems to think," Diana finished. "I don't cringe at a few rough edges."

"Uh, sure," Jervis said, trying and failing not to stare at the noticeable gap that had opened up between Diana's chair and Ten's.

The other cowhands followed Jervis's look. Snickers went around the table like distant lightning, but not one man was going to call down their ramrod's ire by being so rude as to point out that the university woman was politely lying through her pretty white teeth.

Diana didn't notice the looks she received, for she was grimly concentrating on her single pork chop, scant helping of potatoes and no gravy. Despite her usually healthy appetite, her empty stomach and the savory nature of Carla's cooking, Diana was having trouble swallowing. Even though none of the other men at the table were as big as Cash—and Luke wasn't even in the dining room—she felt suffocated by looming, uncivilized, unpredictable males.

"Miss Saxton," Ten continued, "will be here for the summer, working at the September Canyon site." He glanced at the woman, who was at the moment subtly hitching her chair even farther away from him, and drawled, "It *is* Miss, isn't it?"

Carla gave Ten a quick glance, caught by the unusual edge in his normally smooth voice. Then she noticed what the cowhands had already seen—the gap that had slowly opened up between Diana's chair and the ramrod's.

"Actually," Diana said, "my students call me Dr. Saxton and my friends call me Di."

"What does your husband call you?" Ten asked blandly.

"I'm not married."

Ten would have been surprised by any other answer, a fact that he didn't bother to conceal.

"Dr. Diana Saxton," Ten continued, "will be spending most of her time at the September Canyon digs. In between, she'll be living at the old house, which means that you boys better clean up your act. Voices carry real well from the bunkhouse to the old house. Anybody who embarrasses the lady will hear from me."

"And from me," Luke said, pulling out his chair and sitting down. "Pass the pork chops, please." He looked at Diana, saw the gap between her chair and Ten's and gave the ramrod a look that was both amused and questioning. "Didn't you have time to shower before dinner?"

The left corner of Ten's mouth lifted in wry acknowledgment, but he said nothing.

"When are you leaving?" Carla asked quickly, turning toward her brother, Cash. She didn't know why Diana kept edging farther away from Ten but guessed that she would be embarrassed if it were pointed out. By and large the cowhands were kind men, but their humor was both blunt and unrelenting.

"Right after we play poker tonight," Cash said.

"Poker?" Carla groaned.

"Sure. I thought I'd introduce Dr. Saxton to the joys of seven-card stud."

Smiling politely, Diana looked up from her plate. "Thanks, but I'm really tired. Maybe some other time."

The cowhands laughed as though she had made a joke.

"Guess they teach more than stones and bones at that university," Jervis said when the laughter ended. "Must teach some common sense, too."

Diana looked at Carla, who smiled.

"My brother is, er, well . . ." Carla's voice faded.

"Cash is damned lucky at cards," Ten said succinctly. "He'll clean you down to the lint in your pockets."

"It's true," said Carla. "His real name is Alexander, but anyone who has ever played cards with him calls him Cash."

"In fact," Luke said, pouring gravy over mounds of food, "I'm one of the few men in living memory ever to beat Cash at poker."

Cash smiled slightly and examined his dinner as though he expected it to get up and walk off the plate.

"Of course," Luke continued, "Cash cheated."

Cash's head snapped up.

"He wanted Carla to spend the summer on the Rocking M," Luke said matter-of-factly. "So he suckered her into betting a summer's worth of cooking. Cash won, of course. Then he turned around and carefully lost his sister's whole summer to me." Luke ran his fingertip from Carla's cheekbone to the corner of her smile before he turned to Cash and said quietly, "I never thanked you for giving Carla to me, but not a day goes by that I don't thank God."

Diana looked at the two big men and the woman who sat wholly at ease between them, smiling, her love for her husband and her brother as vivid as the blue-green of her eyes. The men's love for her was equally obvious, almost tangible. An odd aching closed Diana's throat, making an already difficult dinner impossible to swallow.

"I hope you know how lucky you are," she said to Carla. Without warning, Diana pushed back from the table and stood. "I'm afraid I'm too tired to eat. If you'll excuse me, I'll make it an early night."

"Of course," Carla said. "If you're hungry later, just come in the back way and eat whatever looks good. Ten does it all the time."

"Thanks," Diana said, already turning away, eager to be gone from the room full of men.

Nobody said a word until Diana had been gone long enough to be well beyond range of their voices. Then Luke turned, raised his eyebrows questioningly and looked straight at Ten.

"Are you the burr under her saddle?" Luke asked.

There was absolute silence as all the cowhands leaned forward to hear the answer to the question none of them had the nerve to ask their ramrod.

"She saw me take down Baker," Ten said. "Shocked her, I guess. Then I made her hold Nosy while I cut that boil. Now she thinks I'm a cross between Attila the Hun and Jack the Ripper."

Luke grunted. "Nice work, by the way. Baker, I mean. Nosy, too, I suppose. Carla was worried about that fool kitten. Me, I think we have too darn many cats as it is."

Luke caught the light, slow-motion blow Carla aimed at his shoulder. He brushed a kiss over her captive hand and said, "Honey, from now on put Diana next to you at the table. If the pretty professor moves her chair any farther away from Ten, we'll have to serve her food in the kitchen."

The cowhands burst out laughing. For a few minutes more the talk centered around the overly shy professor with the striking blue eyes and very nicely rounded body. Then food began to disappear in earnest and conversation slowed. After dessert vanished as well, so did the cowhands. Cash went upstairs to pack, leaving Ten, Luke and Carla alone to enjoy a final cup of coffee before the evening's work of kitchen cleanup and bookkeeping began.

Ten rubbed his jaw thoughtfully and was rewarded by the rasp of beard stubble. Undoubtedly that, too, had counted against him with the wary professor. Which was too bad—it had been a long time since a woman had interested him quite as much as the one with the frightened eyes and a body that would tempt a saint.

"How do you want to divide up Baker's work?" Luke asked Ten.

"I can take the leased grazing lands over on the divide, but that leaves the Wildfire Canyon springs without a hand."

"I'll take the grazing lands and have Jervis camp over at Wildfire Canyon during the week and weekends at September Canyon."

"That will make for long days for you," Ten said, glancing quickly at Carla. He knew that Luke had been trying to spend as much time as possible with his wife and new son.

"Your days will be even longer," Luke said. "Starting tomorrow, you're ramrodding the dig at September Canyon."

"Jervis can do it. He gets along with the university types real well. You'd never know it to listen to him, but he taught math in Oregon before he took up ranch work."

"You'd never know it to listen to you, either," retorted Luke, "but I happen to know a certain ramrod who speaks three languages and who still gets calls in the middle of the night from official types who want advice on how to get sticky jobs unstuck."

Ten said nothing.

"But they're just going to have to wait in line," Luke continued. "I've got all the trouble you can handle right in September Canyon."

Without moving, Ten became fully alert. Luke saw the change and smiled thinly.

"You expecting some kind of trouble at the site?" Ten asked.

Luke looked at Carla. "Don't I hear Logan crying?" he asked.

"Why don't you go and check?" Carla offered.

The look Luke gave Carla plainly said he wished she weren't listening to what he was saying to Ten. She looked right back, plainly telling Luke that she wasn't leaving without a good reason. Reluctantly he smiled, but when he turned to Ten the smile faded.

"The sheriff called," Luke said. "There's a ring of pot-hunters working the Four Corners. They dig during the week and avoid the weekends when there are more people in the back country. They're professional and they're tough."

"How tough?"

"They roughed up some folks over in Utah. The Park Service isn't making any noise about it, but the back-country rangers are going armed these days. So are the pothunters."

"Want me to leave now for the site?" Ten asked.

"No. One of the sheriff's men is camping out that way, unofficially. But he's got to be back on the road early tomorrow."

Into the dining room came the clear sound of an unhappy baby. Carla put her hand on Luke's shoulder and pressed down, silently telling him not to get up.

"I'll leave before dawn," Ten said, watching Carla hurry from the room.

"The professor won't like that."

"I'll be quiet," Ten said dryly.

"Don't bother. She's going with you. That little Japanese rice burner of hers wouldn't get four miles up the pasture road, much less across Picture Wash to September Canyon."

Ten smiled rather wolfishly. "She's not going to like being trapped in a truck with me. Or are you sending Carla to ride shotgun?"

"Nope," Luke said cheerfully. "She's got two full-time jobs riding herd on me and the baby."

"That's the problem. We've all got too damn many full-time jobs and not enough hands."

"I put the word out at every ranch for three hundred miles," Luke said, stretching his long arms over his head. "All we can do is wait. Jason Ironcloud promised he'd start breaking horses as soon as his sister's husband is out of jail. Until then, he's got to take care of her ranch."

"What's the husband in for—the usual?" Ten asked.

"Drunk and disorderly."

"The usual."

Luke grunted agreement.

Ten rubbed his raspy chin thoughtfully. "Nevada called. He's pulling out of Afghanistan. He'll be home in a few weeks."

Luke glanced sideways at Ten. "Is he still a renegade?"

"All the Blackthorns are wild. It's the Highland Scots blood."

"Yeah. Outlaws to the bone. Like you. You don't make any noise about it, but you go your own way and to hell with what the rest of the world thinks."

Ten said only, "A few years of guerrilla warfare tends to settle down even the wildest kid."

"You should know."

"Yes. I should know."

Luke nodded and said softly, "Hire him."

Ten looked at Luke. "Thanks. I owe you one."

"No way, *compadre*. I should have been the man to shake the kinks out of Baker, not you."

A slight smile crossed the ramrod's face. "My pleasure."

Luke looked thoughtful. "Does Nevada fight the same way you do?"

"Wouldn't surprise me. He was taught by the same people."

"Good. He can trade off guarding September Canyon with you." Luke sighed and rubbed his neck wearily. "You know, there are days I wish Carla had never found those damn ruins. It's costing us thousands of dollars a year in manpower alone just to keep pothunters out."

"We could do what some of the other ranchers have done."

"What's that?"

"Sell some of the artifacts to pay for protecting the ruins."

"The September Canyon ruins are on your part of the ranch," Luke said, his face expressionless. "Is that what you want to do?"

Ten shook his head. "I'll give the land back to you before I sell off artifacts. Or I'll give the land back to the government if neither one of us can afford to protect the ruins. My head knows that ninety-eight percent of those artifacts aren't unique—universities and museums are full of Anasazi stuff as good or better. Once the excavation has been carefully done, there's no good reason not to get back the cost of the digging by selling off some of the stuff."

"But?" Luke asked.

Ten shrugged. "But my gut keeps telling me that those artifacts belong in the place where they were made and used and broken and mended and used again. It's pure foolishness but that's how I feel about it, and as long as I can afford it, I plan on keeping my foolish ways."

Luke looked at Ten and said quietly, "If my drunken daddy had sold pieces of the Rocking M to anybody but you, I would have been in a world of hurt with no place to call home."

Ten stood and clapped Luke on the shoulder. "It was an even trade, *compadre*. Back then, I was in a world of hurt and looking for a home."

"You've got the home. What about the hurt? Still have that?"

"I got over it a long time ago."

"Then why haven't you married again?"

"A smart dog doesn't have to be taught the same lesson twice," Ten said sardonically. "I'm a hell of a lot smarter than a dog."

"She must have been something."

"Who?"

"Your ex-wife."

Ten shrugged. "She was honest. That's better than most. When the sex wore off she wanted out. By then I was more than willing. Next time I was smarter. I didn't marry just because my blood was running hot. After a few weeks the same thing happened, only this time the girl didn't want to admit it. I shipped out the first chance I got."

"That was a long time ago. You were a wild kid chasing girls who were no better than they had to be. You're different now."

Ten shook his head, "You got lucky, Luke. I didn't. You learned one thing about women and marriage. I learned another."

Without giving Luke a chance to speak, Ten left the room. Behind him, Luke sat motionless, listening to the sound of Ten's fading footsteps and the soft thump of a closing door.

Four

As the dirt road zigzagged across national forest lease lands and down the steep side of the high, mountainous plateau where the Rocking M ranch buildings were located, the land became more dry and the earth more intensely colored. Gullies became deeper, rocky cliffs more common, and the creeks and rivers widened into broad, often dry washes winding among spectacular stone-walled canyons. Juniper and piñon mixed with sagebrush, giving the air a clean, pungent smell. In deep, protected clefts where tiny springs welled forth, a handful of true pine trees grew next to cottonwoods. Along the canyon bottoms the brush thinned to clumps. Depending on altitude or exposure, juniper, piñon, cedar and big sage grew.

Diana watched the changing landscape intently, seeking the plants that were the hallmark and foundation of Anasazi culture—yucca and piñon, bee plant and goosefoot. On the higher flatlands she also looked for stands of big sage, which grew where the earth had been disturbed and then abandoned by man. Each time another nameless canyon or gully opened up along the rough dirt road, she looked at the unexplored land with a yearning she couldn't disguise.

"Stop it," Ten said finally. "You're making me feel like the Marquis de Sade."

Startled, Diana turned toward him. "What?"

"Don't worry. I'm not talking about the way you hug the door handle as though it were your last hope of safety," Ten drawled, giving her a sideways glance.

A flush crawled up Diana's cheeks. She looked down and saw that she was all but sitting on the door handle in order to get as much distance as possible between herself and Ten.

"I—it's nothing personal," she said, her voice strained.

"Like hell it isn't," Ten said calmly. "But that's not what made me feel like a sadist. It's the way you look at all those canyons that's getting to me. It's the way a starving man looks at food, or a thirsty man looks at water, or Luke looks at Carla when they all sit in the rocking chair while she nurses Logan. If it will make you feel any better, we can stop and get closer to whatever it is you love so much."

Ten's perceptivity startled Diana. It was unexpected in a man. But then, Ten had been unexpected from the first moment she saw him. The longer she was around him, the more unexpected he became.

"That's—that's very kind of you, Mr. Blackthorn, but I'm afraid looking won't make me feel much better."

Clear, ice-gray eyes glanced briefly at Diana, then resumed watching the rough road.

"What would make you feel better, professor?"

"Being called something else, *ramrod,*" she shot back before she could think better of it.

The corner of Ten's mouth tugged up. "I'm not much on formality. Call me Ten."

Diana started to reciprocate, then stopped, afraid that Ten would mistake politeness for an entirely different sort of offer.

He shot her another quick glance. "Go ahead, I won't take it as a come-on."

"I beg your pardon?"

"Go ahead and ask me to call you Diana. I'll assume you're being polite, not looking for a little action."

"Let me assure you, I'm not looking for a 'little action.'"

"I figured that out the first time I saw you. So uncramp your hand from the door handle and tell me why you're looking at the countryside like you're saying goodbye to your only friend."

"Are you always this direct?"

"Yes. Are you always this nervous around men or is it me in particular?"

"Does it matter?"

"If I'm the one setting you on edge, I'll get out of your hair as soon as possible," Ten said matter-of-factly. "If it's just men in general you don't like, it won't matter who's on site with you."

Diana was silent.

"Well that tells me," Ten said, shrugging. "As soon as Nevada arrives, I'll turn September Canyon over to him."

"It's not you," Diana said, forcing out each word.

"Did anyone ever mention that you don't lie worth a damn? You've been terrified of me ever since I came over the corral fence and taught Baker what his horse already knew—in a fight, smart goes farther than big."

Diana closed her eyes, seeing again the blows landing too quickly to be believed. "Fast, strong and lethal count, too. Baker never had a chance, did he?"

"Only a fool, a horse or a woman would give a man like Baker a chance."

"Are you calling me a fool?"

"No. I'm not calling you a horse, either."

She made a strangled sound that was close to laughter, surprising herself.

A quick, sideways glance told Ten that Diana's grip on the door handle had eased. It also told him that her eyes were an even deeper, more brilliant blue than he had thought, and that the curve of her mouth was made to be traced by a man's tongue.

The shadow of another small canyon opening up off the road caught Diana's attention. The hint of laughter that had curved her mouth faded, leaving behind a yearning line.

"What is it that you see?" Ten asked softly.

The words slid past Diana's reflexive defenses and touched the one thing she permitted herself to love, the Anasazi homeland with its mixture of mountains and mesas and canyons, sandstone and shale, its violent summer storms, and the massive silence that made her feel as though time itself flowed through the ancient canyons.

"That canyon off to the right," Diana said, pointing to a place where a crease opened up at the base of a mesa. "Does it have a name?"

"Not that I know of."

"That's what I thought. There are hundreds of canyons like it on the Colorado Plateau. Thousands. And in each one, it would be unusual to walk more than a mile along the mesa top or the canyon bottom without finding some legacy of the Anasazi, such as broken pots or masonry or ruined stone walls."

Ten made a startled sound and glanced quickly at Diana.

"It's true," she said, turning to face him. "The Colorado Plateau is one of the richest archaeological areas of the world. Some experts say that there are a hundred archaeological sites per square mile. Others say a hundred and twenty sites. Naturally, all of the sites aren't important enough to excavate, but the sheer number of them is amazing. For instance, in Montezuma County alone, there are probably one hundred *thousand* archaeological sites."

Ten whistled through his teeth. The boyish gesture both startled and intrigued Diana, for it was so much at odds with the fierce man who had fought Baker and the quiet man who had treated a sick kitten with such care.

"How many Anasazi lived around here, anyway?" Ten asked.

"Here? I don't know. But over in Montezuma Valley there were about thirty thousand people. That's greater than the population today. It's the same for the rest of the Colorado Plateau. At the height of the Anasazi culture, the land supported more people than it does today with twentieth-century technology.

"And up every nameless canyon," Diana continued, her voice husky with emotion, "there's a chance of finding the one extraordinary ruin that will explain why the Anasazi culture thrived in this area for more than ten centuries and then simply vanished without warning, as though the people picked up in the middle of a meal and left, taking nothing with them."

"That's what you're looking for? The answer to an old mystery?"

She nodded.

"Why?"

The question startled Diana. "What do you mean?"

"What is it you really want?" Ten asked. "Glory? Wealth? A tenured job at an eastern university? Classrooms full of students who think you're smarter than God?"

"Is it academia in general you dislike or me in particular?"

Ten heard the echo of his own previous question and smiled to himself. "I don't know you well enough to dislike you. I'm just curious."

"So am I," Diana said tightly. "That's why I want to know about the Anasazi. Their abrupt disappearance from the cliff houses at the height of their cultural success is as big a mystery as what really caused the extinction of dinosaurs."

She glanced covertly at Ten. Though he was watching the rough, difficult road, she sensed that he was listening closely to her words. Despite her usual reticence on the subject of herself, there was something about Ten that made her want to keep talking, if only to give him a better opinion of her than he obviously had. Not that she could really blame him for being cool toward her; she had done everything but crawl under the table to avoid him at dinner.

The contrasts and contradictions of the man called Tennessee Blackthorn both intrigued and irritated Diana. A man who could fight with such savage efficiency shouldn't also care about sick kittens. A man who could handle the physical demands of the big truck and the rotten road with such effortless skill shouldn't be so interested in something as abstract and intangible as the vanished Anasazi, yet he had shown obvious interest every time the subject had come up.

But most of all, a man who was so abrasively masculine shouldn't have been perceptive enough to notice her silent yearning after unexplored canyons. Nor should she be noticing right now the clean line of his profile, the high forehead and thick, faintly curling pelt of black hair, the luxuriant black eyelashes and crystal clarity of his eyes, the subdued sensuality of his mouth.

The direction of Diana's thoughts made her distinctly uneasy. She turned and looked out the window again, yet it was impossible for her to go back to the long silences of the previous hours in the truck when she had tried to shut out the presence of everything except the land.

"As for prestige or a tenured teaching position," Diana continued, looking out the window, "I'm not a great candidate for any university, especially an eastern one. I love the Colorado Plateau country too much to live anywhere else. I stand in front of classrooms full of students—worshipful or otherwise—because teaching gives me the money and time to explore the Anasazi culture in the very places where the Ancient Ones once lived, and then make what I've seen and learned come alive in drawings.''

"You're an artist?"

Short, golden brown hair rippled and shone in the sun as Diana shook her head in a silent negative. "At best, I'm an illustrator. I take the site photographer's pictures, read the archaeological summaries of the site and study the artifacts that have been excavated. Then I combine everything with my own knowledge of the Anasazi and make a series of drawings of the site as it probably looked when it was inhabited."

"Sounds like more than illustration to me."

"I assure you, it's less than art. My mother is an artist, so I know the difference."

"Do your parents live in Colorado?"

"My mother lives in Arizona."

Normally Ten would have let the matter of parents drop, especially since Diana's voice had planted warning flags around the subject, but his curiosity about Diana Saxton wasn't normal. She showed flashes of passion coupled with unusual reserve. And it was reserve rather than shyness. Ten had known more than a few shy cowboys. Not one of them would have been able to get up in front of a room full of people and say a single word, much less teach a whole course.

Diana wasn't shy of people. She was shy of men. Ten had immediately figured out that she didn't much care for the male half of the human race. What he hadn't figured out was why.

"What about your father?" Ten asked.

"What about him?"

Though Diana's voice was casual, Ten noted the subtle tightening of her body.

"Where does he live?" Ten asked.

"I don't know."

"Is he why you don't like men?"

"Frankly, it's none of your business."

"Of course it is. I'm a man."

"Mr. Blackthorn—"

"Ten," he interrupted.

"—whether I hate or love men is irrelevant to you or any other man I meet."

"I'll agree about the other men, but not me."

"Why?"

"I'm the man you're going to spend the next five days alone with."

"What?" Diana asked, staring at Ten.

"One of the grad students broke his ankle climbing up a canyon wall," Ten said. Without pausing in his explanations, he whipped the truck around a washout on one side of the road and then a landslide ten yards farther down. "Another one got a job in Illinois working on Indian mounds. The other three can come out only on the weekends because they work during the week."

"So?"

"So I'm staying at the September Canyon site with you."

"That's not necessary. I've been alone at remote digs before."

"Not on the Rocking M you haven't. There will be an armed guard on the site at all times." Without altering his tone at all he said, "Hang on, this will get greasy."

The relaxed lines on Ten's body didn't change as he held the truck on a slippery segment of road where sandstone gave way to thin layers of shale that were so loosely bonded they washed away in even a gentle rain. During the summer season of cloudbursts, the parts of the road that crossed shale formations became impassable for hours or days. Nor was the sandstone itself any treat for driving. Wet sandstone was surprisingly slick.

"There are professional pothunters in the area," Ten continued. "They've worked over a lot of sites. If someone objects, they work them over, too. Luke and I decided that no one goes to September Canyon without a guard."

"Why wasn't I told this before I was hired?" Diana asked tightly.

"Because the sheriff didn't tell us until last night."

Diana said something beneath her breath.

Ten glanced sideways at her. "If you can't handle it, tell me now. We'll be back at the ranch in time for dinner."

She said nothing, still trying to cope with her seething feelings at the thought of being alone with Ten in a remote canyon for five days.

"If I thought it would do any good," Ten said, "I'd give you my word that I won't touch you. But you don't know me well enough to believe me, so there's not much point in making any promises, is there?"

Diana didn't answer.

Without warning Ten brought the truck to a stop in the center of a wide spot in the road. He set the brake and turned to face his unhappy passenger.

"What will it be?" he asked. "September Canyon or back to the ranch house?"

Almost wildly Diana glanced around the countryside. She had been so excited when Carla had offered employment for the summer. The salary was minimal, but the opportunity to study newly discovered ruins was unparalleled.

And now it was all vanishing like rain in the desert.

She looked at Ten. Part of her was frankly terrified at the prospect of being alone with him for days on end. Part of her was not—and in some ways, that was most terrifying of all.

Shutting out everything, Diana closed her eyes. *What am I going to do?*

The image of Ten's powerful hands holding the kitten with such care condensed in her mind.

Surely Carla wouldn't send me out here alone with a man she didn't trust. After that thought came another. *My father was never that gentle with anything. Nor was Steve.*

The ingrained habit of years made Diana's mind veer away from the bleak night when she had learned once and forever to distrust men and her own judgment. Yet she had been luckier than many of the women she had talked with since. Her scars were all on the inside.

Unbidden came a thought that made Diana tremble with a tangle of emotions she refused to name and a question she shouldn't ask, even in the silence of her own mind.

Would Ten be as gentle with a woman as he was with that kitten?

Five

Ten sat and watched the emotions fighting within Diana—anger, fear, hope, confusion, curiosity, longing. The extent of Diana's reluctance to go on to September Canyon surprised him. He had glimpsed the depth of her passion for the Anasazi; if she were considering turning and walking away from September Canyon, she must be in the grip of a fear that was very real to her, despite the fact that Ten knew of no reason for that fear. While most women might have been initially uneasy at spending time alone with a stranger in a remote place, their instinctive wariness would have been balanced by the knowledge that their unexpected companion was a man who had the respect and trust of the people he lived among.

That fact, however, didn't seem to make much difference to Diana.

"Can you talk about it?" Ten asked finally.

"What?"

"Why you're afraid of men. Is it your father?"

Diana looked at Ten's searching, intent eyes, sensing the intelligence and the strength of will in him reaching out to her, asking her to trust him.

Abruptly she felt hemmed in, required to do something for which she was unprepared.

"Stop hounding me," Diana said through clenched teeth. "You have no right to my secrets any more than any man has a right to my body!"

For an instant there was an electric silence stretching tightly between Ten and Diana; then he turned away from her to look out over the land. The silence lengthened until the idling of the truck's engine was as loud as thunder. When Ten finally turned back toward Diana his face was expressionless, his eyes were hooded, and his voice held none of the mixture of emotions it had before.

"In an hour or less those clouds will get together and rain very hard. Then Picture Wash will become impassable. Anyone who is at the September Canyon site will be forced to stay there. Which will it be, Dr. Saxton? Forward to the dig or back to the ranch?"

Ten's voice was even, uninflected, polite. It was like having a stranger ask her for the time of day.

Bitterly Diana reminded herself that Ten was a stranger. Yet somehow he hadn't seemed like one until just now. From the moment Ten had held out the injured kitten to Diana, he had treated her as though she were an old friend newly discovered. She hadn't even realized the... warmth... of his presence until it had been withdrawn.

Now she had an absurd impulse to reach out and touch Ten, to protest the appearance of the handsome, self-contained stranger who waited for her answer with cool attention, his whole attitude telling her that whether she chose to go forward or back, it made no personal difference to him.

"September Canyon," Diana said after a minute. Although she tried, her voice wasn't as controlled as his had been.

Ten took off the brake and resumed driving.

Eventually the silence, which Diana had welcomed before, began to eat at her nerves. She looked out the window but found herself glancing again and again toward Ten. She told herself that it was only his casual skill with the truck that fascinated her. She had done enough rough-country travel in the past to admire his expertise. And it was his expertise she was admiring, not the subtle flex and play of his muscles beneath the faded black work shirt he wore.

"You're a very good driver," she said.

Ten nodded indifferently.

Silence returned, lengthened, filling the cab until Diana rolled down the window just to hear the whistle of wind. She told herself the lack of conversation didn't bother her. After all, she had been the one to resist talk during the long hours since dawn. When Ten had pointed out something along the road or asked about her work, she had nodded or answered briefly and had no questions of her own to offer.

But now that she thought about it, she had a perfect right to ask a few businesslike questions of Ten and get a few businesslike answers.

"Will it distract you to talk?" she asked finally.

"No."

Brief and to the point. Very businesslike. Irritating, too. Silently Diana asked herself if her earlier, brief, impersonal answers had seemed cool and clipped to Ten.

"I didn't mean to be rude earlier," she said.

"You weren't."

Diana waited.

Ten said nothing more.

"How much farther is it to September Canyon?" she asked after a few minutes.

"An hour."

Diana looked up toward the mesa top where piñon and juniper and cedar grew, punctuated by pointed sprays of yucca plants. The clouds had become a solid mass whose bottom was a blue color so deep it was nearly black.

"Looks like rain," she said.

Ten nodded.

More silence, more bumps, more growling sounds from the laboring four-wheel-drive truck.

"Why is it called Picture Wash?" Diana asked in a combination of irritation and determination.

"There are pictographs on the cliffs."

Six whole words. Incredible.

"Anasazi?" she asked.

Ten shrugged.

"Did other Indians live here when the white man came?" Diana asked, knowing very well that they had.

Ten nodded.

"Mountain Utes?" she asked, again knowing the answer.

"Yes," he said as he swerved around a mass of shale that had extended a slippery tongue onto the roadway.

Diana hardly noticed the evasive maneuver. She was intent on drawing out the suddenly laconic Ten. Obviously that would require a question that couldn't be answered by yes, no or a shrug. Inspiration came.

"Why are you called Tennessee?"

"I was the oldest."

"I don't understand."

"Neither did Dad."

Diana gave up the word game and concentrated on the land.

The truck kicked and twitched and skidded around a series of steep, uphill curves, climbing up a mesa spur and onto the top. There was a long, reasonably straight run across the spur. Piñon and juniper whipped by, interspersed with a handful of big sage and other drought-adapted shrubs.

Abruptly there was an opening in the piñon and juniper. Though the ground looked no different, big sagebrush grew head-high and higher. Their silver-gray, twisting branches were thicker than a strong man's arm.

"Stop!" Diana said urgently.

The truck shuddered to a halt. Before the pebbles scattered by the tires finished rolling, Diana had her seat belt off and was jumping down the cab.

"What's wrong?" Ten asked, climbing out of the truck.

Diana didn't answer. Watching the ground with intent, narrowed eyes, she quartered the stand of big sage, twisting and turning, zigzagging across the open areas in the manner of someone searching for something. She was so involved in her quest that she didn't seem to notice the scrapes and scratches the rough brush delivered to her unprotected arms.

Ten hesitated at the edge of the road, wondering if Diana was looking for a little privacy. It had been a long drive from the ranch, and there were no amenities such as gas stations or public rest rooms along the way. Yet Diana seemed more interested in the open areas between clumps of big sage than in the thicker growths that would have offered more privacy.

Without warning Diana went down on her knees and began digging hurriedly in the rocky ground. Ten started toward her, ignoring the slap and drag of brush over his clothes. When he was within ten feet of her, she gave a cry of triumph and lifted a squarish rock in both hands. Dirt clung to the edges and dappled light fell across the stone's surface, camouflaging its oddly regular shape.

"Look!" she cried, holding up her prize to Ten.

He eased forward until her was close to her, ducked a branch that had been going after his eyes, straightened and looked.

"A stone," Ten said neutrally.

Diana didn't notice his lack of enthusiasm. She had enough for both of them and the truck, as well. Nor did she

notice the dirty streaks left on her jeans when she rubbed the
rock back and forth, cleaning the part of the stone that had
been buried beneath the dirt. After a few moments she held
the rock in a patch of sunlight coming through the open
branches of the sage.

"Beautiful," she crooned, running her fingertips delicately along the stone, absorbing the subtle variations in the
surface, marks that were the result of applied intelligence
rather than random weathering. "Just . . . beautiful."

The throaty timbre of Diana's voice lured Ten as no stone
could have. He sat on his heels next to her and looked
closely at the rock that she was continuing to stroke as
though it were alive.

The contours of the stone were too even, its edges too
angular to be the result of chance. When the light touched
the rock just right, tiny dimples could be seen, marks left by
countless patient blows from a stone ax held in the hands of
an Anasazi stone mason. Seeing those tangible marks of a
long-dead man made the skin on Ten's skull tighten in a
primal reflex that was far older than the civilized artifact
Diana was cherishing in her hands.

Without realizing it, Ten stretched out his own hand,
feeling a need to confirm the stone's reality through touch.
The rock had the texture of medium sandpaper. The dimples were shallow, more a vague pattern than true pock-
marks. Cold from the ground on one end, sun warmed on
the other, bearing the marks of man all over its surface, the
stone was enduring testimony to a culture that was known
only by its fragmentary ruins.

"How did you know this was here?" Ten asked.

"No juniper or piñon," Diana said absently as she turned
the relic of the past over and over in her hands.

Ten glanced around. She was right. Despite the luxuriant
growth of big sage on the ground, there were no junipers or
piñons for fifty yards in any direction.

"They don't grow on ground that has been disturbed,"
Diana continued, measuring the area of the big sage with

her eyes. "When you see a place like this, there's a very good chance that Anasazi ruins lie beneath the surface, covered by the debris of time and rain and wind."

Gray eyes narrowed while Ten silently reviewed his knowledge of the surrounding countryside.

"There are a lot of patches of big sage on Wind Mesa," he said after a minute. "My God, there must be hundreds of places like this on both sides of Picture Wash. That and the presence of year-round water is why the MacKenzies bought rights to this land more than a century ago."

"It was the water and the presence of game that attracted the Anasazi a thousand years ago. Human needs never change. All that changes is how we express those needs."

With the care of a mother returning a baby to its cradle, Diana replaced the rock in its hollow and smoothed dirt back in place.

"That's what is so exciting about the whole area of Wind Mesa," she said as she worked. "For a long time we believed that the Durango River was the farthest northern reach of the Anasazi in Colorado. September Canyon proved that we were wrong."

"Not all that wrong," Ten said dryly. "You talk as though we're a hundred miles from the river. We're not. It just seems like it by the time you loop around mountains and canyons on these rough roads."

Absently, Diana nodded. When she stood up, she was quite close to Ten. She didn't even notice. Her attention was on the area defined by the silvery big sage, and she was looking at her surroundings with an almost tangible hunger.

"This could have been a field tended by a family and watered by spreader dams and ditches built by the Anasazi," she said. "Or it could have been a small community built near a source of good water and food. It could have been the Anasazi equivalent of a church or a convent or a men's club.

It could have been so many things...and I doubt if we'll ever know exactly what."

"Why not?"

Diana turned and focused on Ten with blue eyes that were as dark and as deep as the storm condensing across the western sky.

"This is Rocking M land," Diana said simply. "Private land. Luke MacKenzie is already bearing the cost of excavating and protecting the September Canyon ruins. I doubt that he can afford to make a habit of that kind of generosity."

"Luke's partner is absorbing the cost, but you're right. Ranching doesn't pay worth a damn as it is. The cost of protecting the whole of Wind Mesa..." Ten lifted his Stetson and resettled it with a jerk. "We'd do it if we could, but we can't. It would bankrupt us."

The sad understanding in Diana's smile said more about regret and acceptance than any words could have.

"Even the government can't afford it," she agreed, rubbing her hands absently on her jeans. "County, state, federal, it doesn't matter which level of government you appeal to. There just isn't enough money. Even at Mesa Verde, which is designed to be a public showcase of the whole range of Anasazi culture, archaeologists have uncovered ruins, measured them, then backfilled them with dirt. It was the only way to protect them from wind, rain and pothunters."

Ten looked around the rugged mesa top and said quietly, "Maybe that's best. Whatever is beneath the earth has been buried for centuries. A few more centuries won't make any difference."

"Here, probably not," Diana said, gesturing to the big sage. "But on the cliffs or on the edges of the mesa, the ruins that aren't buried are disintegrating or being dismantled by pothunters. That's why the work in September Canyon is so important. What we don't learn from it now probably won't be available to learn later. The ruins will have been picked over, packed up and shipped out to private collections all over the world."

The passion and regret in Diana's voice riveted Ten. He was reaching out to touch her in silent comfort when he caught himself. A touch from a man she feared would hardly be a comfort.

"Don't sell this countryside short when it comes to protecting its own," Ten said. "The big sage may be a giveaway on Wind Mesa, but this is a damned inconvenient place to get to. There's only one road and half the time it's impassable. There's a horse trail through the mountains that drops down to September Mesa, but only a few Rocking M riders even know about it and no one has used it in years."

Slowly, almost unwillingly, Diana focused on Ten, sensing his desire to comfort her as clearly as the kitten had sensed its safety within Ten's hands.

"As for the scores of little canyons that might hold cliff ruins," Ten said, watching Diana, sensing the soft uncurling of her tightly held trust, "most of those canyons haven't seen a man since the Anasazi left. Any man. The Utes avoided the ruins as spirit places. Cows avoid the small canyons because the going is too rough, so cowhands don't go there, either. What's hidden stays hidden."

Ten's deep voice with its subtle velvet rasp swirled around Diana, holding her still even as it caressed her. She stared at the clear depths of his eyes and felt a curious mix of hunger and wariness, yearning and . . . familiarity.

"And if some of those ruins are never found, is that so bad?" Ten asked softly. He spoke slowly, watching Diana's eyes, trying to explain something he had never put into words. "Like the Anasazi, the ruins came from time and the land. It's only right that some of them return to their beginnings untouched by any but Anasazi hands."

A throaty muttering of thunder rode the freshening wind. The sound seeped into Diana's awareness, bringing with it a dizzying feeling of déjà vu; of overlapping realities; of time, like a deck of cards, being reshuffled, and the sound

of that shuffling was muted thunder. Her breathing slowed
and then stopped as an eerie certainty condensed within her:
*she had known Ten before, had stood on a mesa top with
him before, had walked with him through piñon and sun
and silence, had slept next to his warmth while lightning and
rain renewed the land....*

The feeling passed, leaving Diana shaken, disoriented,
staring at a man who should have been a stranger and was
not. Thunder came again, closer, insistent. She took a deep
breath, infusing herself with the elemental, unforgettable
pungency of sage and piñon, juniper and storm. And time.
That most of all. The scent of time and a storm coming
down.

Closing her eyes, Diana breathed deeply, filling herself
with the storm wind, feeling it touch parts of her that had
been curled tightly shut for too many years. The sensation
of freedom and vulnerability that followed was frightening
and exhilarating at the same time, like swimming nude in a
midnight lake.

"Storm coming," Ten said, looking away from Diana
because if he watched her drink the wind any longer he
wouldn't be able to stop himself from touching her. "If
we're going to cross Picture Wash, we have to hurry. Unless
you've changed your mind?"

Diana's eyes opened. She saw a powerful man standing
motionless, silhouetted against sunlight and thunderheads,
his head turned away from her. Then he looked back at her,
and his eyes were like cut crystal against the darkness of his
face.

"Diana?"

The sound of her name on Ten's lips made sensations
glitter through her body from breastbone to knees.

"Yes," she said, trying to sound businesslike and failing. "I'm coming."

Six

There was some water running in Picture Wash, but the big ranch truck crossed without difficulty. Splash marks on the other side of the ford told Ten that he wasn't the only person who had driven toward September Canyon today. Ten glanced quickly around but saw nothing. They had passed no one the entire length of the one-lane dirt road, which meant that the other vehicle was still in front of them.

Frowning, Ten turned right and drove along the edge of the broad wash. There was no real road to follow, simply a suggestion of tire tracks where other vehicles had gone before. Tributary canyons opened up on the left of the wash, and more were visible across the thin ribbon of water, but Ten made no attempt to explore those openings. After three miles he turned left into the mouth of a side canyon.

Diana looked at him questioningly.

"September Canyon," Ten said. "The mesa it's eaten out of didn't really have a name, but we've started calling it

September Mesa since we've been working on the site. Wind Mesa is behind us now, across the wash."

"What's upstream?"

"More canyons. Smaller. If you follow the wash upstream long enough, it finally narrows into a crack and disappears against a wall of stone, which is the body of the mesa itself. Almost all the canyons are blind. Only one or two have an outlet on top of the mesa. Other than that, the canyons are a maze. Even with a compass, it's hard not to get lost."

Diana turned around, trying to orient herself. "Where is the Rocking M?"

Ten gestured with his head because he needed both hands for the wheel. "North and east, on top of the big mesa."

"It is? I thought the ranch was on the edge of a broad valley."

He smiled slightly. "So do most people who come on the Rocking M from the north. You don't know the valley is really a mesa until you drive off the edge. The mountains confuse you. All of the Colorado Plateau is like that."

Diana reached into her back jeans pocket, pulled out a United States Geological Survey map and began searching for the vague line that represented the ranch road they were on. The bouncing of the truck made map reading impossible.

"Perspective is a funny thing," Ten said, glancing at the map for an instant. "Coming in from the south and east, you see the wall of the mesa, the cliffs and gorges and canyons. That's where the explorers were when they started naming things—at the bottom looking up. You can't see the Fire Mountains from that angle, and everything looks dark and jumbled at a distance, so the whole area was once called Black Plateau or Fire Mountain Plateau, depending on which old-timer you talk to."

Diana folded up the map and put it away.

"On the other hand," Ten continued, "if you're coming in from the mountain end of the territory, you see a mesa top as more of a broad valley, and you name it accordingly."

"Is that what happened on the Rocking M?"

Ten nodded. "Case MacKenzie started out with a ranch at the base of what became known as MacKenzie Ridge, which is a foothill of the Fire Mountains. From his perspective, the mesa top is a broad, winding valley. But history named the hunk of land for a hundred miles in all directions Black Plateau, even though it's more like a mesa than a plateau. Then you add a hundred years of Spanish and American cowboys translating Indian names and adding their own to the mix, and you have a mapmaker's nightmare."

"You also have a lot of lost tourists."

The left corner of Ten's mouth lifted slightly. "Just remember that September Mesa and Wind Mesa and all the nameless mesas are nothing but narrow fingers stretching out from the huge hand known as Black Plateau or MacKenzie Valley, depending on which direction your mapmaker came from."

"I'm beginning to understand why men invented satellite photos. It's the only way to see how the pieces all fit together."

Ten shot Diana an amused, approving glance, but only for an instant. The truck, moving at barely five miles an hour, bumped and thumped over the rock-strewn, narrowing canyon bottom. To Diana's eyes there was nothing to distinguish the cliff-rimmed canyon they had entered from the many other tributary canyons that emptied into Picture Wash. The mouth of September Canyon was perhaps eighty yards across, marked by nothing but a faint suggestion of tire tracks in the sand. The cliffs were of a vaguely ruddy, vaguely gold sandstone that overlay narrower beds of shale. The shale crumbled readily, forming steep, slippery talus slopes at the base of the sandstone cliffs.

Scattered on the surface of the gray-brown shale debris were huge, erratic piles of sandstone rubble that were formed when the shale crumbled and washed away faster than the more durable cliffs above, leaving the sandstone cliffs without support at their base. Then great sheets of sandstone peeled away from the overhanging cliffs and fell to the earth below, shattering into rubble and leaving behind arches and alcoves and deeper overhangs—and, sometimes, filling pre-existing alcoves.

In many cases the shale had been eroded by the seeping of groundwater between layers of sandstone and shale. When the water eventually reached the edge of a cliff or a ravine, it became a spring, a source of clean, year-round water for the people who eventually sought shelter in the arching overhangs that the springs had helped to create. Without the water there would have been no cliff-hanging alcoves for men to take shelter within, no easily defended villages set into sheer stone. Without the very special circumstances of sandstone, shale and water, the Anasazi civilization would have developed very differently, if it developed at all.

That interlocking of Anasazi and the land had always fascinated Diana. The fact that their cliff houses were found in some of the most remote, starkly beautiful landscapes in America simply added to her fascination.

"Does the Rocking M run cattle here?" Diana asked.

"Not for several years."

"Then how were the ruins discovered?"

"Carla was returning a potshard that Luke had found years ago in the mouth of September Canyon and given to her. She drove out from Boulder alone and spent several hours walking the canyon floor. There had been a storm recently and a tree had fallen. She came around a bend and there the ruins were."

"That must have been incredible," Diana said, her voice throaty with longing.

"I doubt that Carla was in a mood to appreciate it. She had come here to say goodbye to everything she had ever wanted—the land, the ranch, and most of all the man."

"Luke?"

Ten nodded.

"What changed her mind?"

"Luke. He finally got it through his hard head that Carla was the one woman in a million who could live on an isolated ranch and not go sour."

Diana's mouth turned down in a sad curve. "I was ranch-raised. It's not for everyone, man or woman."

"You didn't like it?"

"I loved it. No matter how bad things at home got, the land was always waiting, always beautiful, always there. I could walk away from the buildings and the land would..." Her voice shivered into silence as she realized what she had almost revealed.

"Heal you?" Ten suggested softly.

Diana's eyes closed and a tiny shudder went through her. Ten was too perceptive. He saw things with dangerous clarity.

"The land was here long before a primate climbed down out of a tree and put a kink in his back trying to see over the grass," Ten said matter-of-factly. "The land will be here long after we're gone. That frightens some people because it makes them feel small and worthless. But some people are made whole by touching something that's bigger than they are, something enduring, something that lives on a different time scale than man."

The words slid past Diana's defenses, making her realize that Ten was one of those who had come to the land to be healed.

"What hurt you?" she asked before she could stop herself.

The lines of Ten's face shifted, reminding Diana of the cold, deadly fighter who had come over the corral fence and flattened a larger, whip-wielding opponent in a matter of seconds.

"I'm sorry," Diana said quickly. "I had no right to ask."

Ten nodded curtly, either agreeing with her or accepting her apology, she wasn't certain which.

It was silent in the truck for a few moments before Ten said, "We're coming up on the base camp. It's beneath that big overhang on the left."

Diana heard more than the words; she heard what wasn't said, as well. Gone was the subtle emotion that had made Ten's voice like black velvet when he talked about the land. His tone was neither reserved nor outgoing, simply neutral. Polite.

Telling herself that Ten's withdrawal didn't matter, Diana looked beyond his handsome, unyielding profile to the smooth cliff wall rising above scattered piñons. The sandstone gleamed against the thunderheads that had consumed the sky. Something bright flickered at the edge of her vision. A few seconds later thunder pealed through the narrow canyon, shaking the ground. Spectral light flickered and danced again, and again thunder reverberated between stone walls.

Diana closed her eyes and breathed in deeply, savoring the pungent, suddenly cool wind. Soon it would begin to rain. She could feel it. She could smell it in the air, the unique blend of heat and dust rising up from the ground and countless water drops reaching down to caress the dry land.

Thunder belled again and then again. A gust of wind came through the open truck window, pouring over Diana. She laughed softly, wishing she were alone so that she could hold out her arms and embrace the wild summer storm.

The subdued music of Diana's laughter drew Ten's attention. He looked at her for only an instant, but it was enough. He knew he would never forget the picture she made with her head thrown back and her hair tousled as though by a lover's hands, her cheeks flushed with excitement and her lips parted as she gave herself to the storm wind.

The persistent male curiosity Ten had felt at his first sight of Diana retreating from the skirmish at the corral became a torrent of desire pouring through him, hardening him with a speed he hadn't known since he was a teenager. Cursing silently, he forced his attention away from his quickened body and onto the demands of the terrain. The last quarter of a mile to the ruins was tricky, because most of it was over greasy shale slopes studded with house-size boulders of sandstone that had fallen from the thick, cliff-forming layer of rock. The truck bucked and tires spun in protest at the slippery going as the vehicle groaned up the final hill.

"Wouldn't it have been better to walk from the base camp?" Diana asked, bracing herself against the dashboard.

"I was in a hurry."

"Why?" she asked, looking toward him as the truck bucked over the ridge and stopped abruptly.

"That's why."

The flat, predatory quality of Ten's voice froze Diana's breath. Slowly she followed his glance.

A dirty Range Rover was parked among the rubble at the base of the cliff. Beyond the vehicle, lightweight aluminum ladders extended up the twenty feet of massive sandstone that separated the ruins from the rubble below.

Ten reached over, unlocked the gun rack that hung over the rear window and chose the shotgun, leaving the rifle in place. He checked the shotgun's load, racked a shell into the chamber, then got out of the truck and closed the door before he turned to look at Diana through the open window.

"Stay here."

Thunder belled harshly, followed by a cannonade of rain sweeping in shining veils over the ground. Holding the shotgun muzzle down, Ten ignored the rain that quickly soaked through his clothing. There was a muffled shout from the ruins. He ignored that, too. The Range Rover was unlocked. He went through the vehicle quickly, finding and unloading a pistol and a rifle. A quick motion of his wrist sent bullets arcing out into the rain. The weapons he put way in the back of the Rover, next to a big carton. With one eye on the pothunters who were scrambling down the rain-slick ladders, Ten ripped open the box.

It was filled with Anasazi pots, their bold geometries and corrugated finish unmistakable in the watery light. Bits of turquoise and shell gleamed in the bottom of one bowl. Ten lifted the carton out, set it on the ground and returned to the interior of the Rover. It stank of cigarette smoke and gasoline that was evaporating from a five-gallon container with a faulty seal.

As the pothunters hit the bottom of the ladder and started running toward him, Ten opened the container and pushed it over inside the car. The stench of raw gas swirled up, overpowering.

"Hey!" hollered the first man. "Get the hell out of there! That car's private property!"

The Rover was between Ten and the pothunters. When he stepped out around the rear of the Rover, the men could see the shotgun held with professional ease in Ten's hands, muzzle slanted down, neither pointing toward nor away from the men.

The first man slowed his reckless pace to a wary walk. He was in his mid-twenties and carried himself as though he had spent time in the military. He was big, hard-shouldered, used to intimidating people with his sheer size.

"You're trespassing on Rocking M land," Ten said.

"I didn't see any signs."

The line of Ten's mouth lifted in a sardonic curl. "Too bad. Get in your Rover and drive out of here."

The other two men caught up with the first just as he shouted, "You'll be hearing from me, cowboy. You're threatening private citizens. We were just traveling around in the back country and made a wrong turn somewhere. It could have happened to anyone—and that's what I'll tell the sheriff when I file a complaint!"

"The only wrong turn you made was in thinking all you'd find out here were pots and a few grad students even younger than you."

"Think you're a big man with that shotgun, don't you?"

"You sure didn't learn much in the marines before they threw you out."

"How did you know I was..." The man's voice faded even as angry color rose in his face. He jerked his head toward the Rover. The other two men reached for the door handles.

Ten watched with an air of shuttered expectancy. He wasn't disappointed. No sooner did the two men open the Rover's doors than there were simultaneous shouts of outrage.

"He poured gas all over the damn car!"

"Milt, the pots are gone!"

Then one of the men noticed the guns. He slammed the door and said in disgust, "Pack it in, Milt. He got to the guns."

Milt's face flattened into mean lines as he measured the cowboy standing at ease in front of him.

"You heard them," Ten said. "Pack it in." He raised his voice slightly and said to the other two men, "Get in the Rover and shut the doors."

The younger man colored with frustration and anger when his two companions obediently climbed into the Rover, slamming both doors hard behind them.

"Those are my pots," Milt said angrily. "If they're not in the Rover when I leave, I'll sue your smart ass for theft."

"Go home, kid. School's out."

As Ten spoke, he casually broke open the shotgun and removed the shell from the firing chamber.

Milt was as foolish as Ten had hoped. The younger man began weaving and feinting, his body held in the stance of someone who had been trained in unarmed combat.

Ten closed the shotgun with a fast snap of his wrist and set the weapon on the Rover's hood before he turned and walked toward the younger man. As though Ten's calm approach unnerved Milt, he attacked. Ten deflected the charge with a deceptively casual motion of his shoulders that sent Milt staggering off balance over the slippery rubble. He went to his hands and knees, then scrambled to his feet and came after Ten again.

One of the Rover's doors opened just behind Ten. He spun around and lashed out with his booted foot, connecting with metal. There was a startled curse, a cry of pain and the sound of the door slamming closed beneath Ten's foot. Before the echo could return from the stone walls, Ten had turned around again.

Milt was more careful in his tactics this time, but the result was still the same. When he lunged for Ten, Milt got nothing but a handful of mud. It happened again, then a fourth time, and each time Milt ended up on his hands and knees.

"Hurry up, kid," Ten said, watching Milt push to his feet for the fifth time. "I'm getting tired of standing around in the rain waiting for you to get smart."

With an inarticulate cry of rage, Milt came to his feet, clawing beneath his windbreaker with his right hand, tearing a hunting knife free of its sheath. This time when Milt charged, Ten made a single swift movement that sent the other man head over heels to land hard and flat on his back, gasping for air. Ten's boot descended on Milt's right wrist. Bending over, Ten took the knife from Milt's hand, tested the edge of the blade and made a disdainful sound.

"You'd be lucky to cut butter with this, boy."

Milt's glazed eyes focused on Ten, who was throwing the knife from hand to hand, flipping it end over end, testing the knife's balance with the expertise of someone thoroughly accustomed to using a knife as a weapon.

"Other than the edge, it's a nice knife," Ten said after a few moments. "Really fine."

There was a brief blur of movement followed by the sound of steel grating through earth. Buried half the length of its blade, the knife gleamed only inches from Milt's shocked face. Ten removed his boot from Milt's wrist.

"Pull the knife out and put it back in your belt."

Milt reached slowly for the knife. For an instant as his fingers closed around the hilt, he thought of throwing the knife at the smaller, rain-soaked man who had humiliated him with such offhanded ease.

Watching with the clear-eyed patience of a predator, Ten waited to see how smart Milt was.

Slowly, reluctantly, Milt returned the knife to its sheath.

"You're learning, kid. Too bad. I was looking forward to watching you eat that knife." Ten bent down and dragged the younger man to his feet with a single powerful motion. "Now here's something else for you to learn. I've been hearing things about a busted-out gyrene pothunter who gets his kicks slapping around teachers whose only crime is wanting to camp in a national park."

For the first time since the fight had started, Milt was close enough to see Ten's eyes beneath the dripping brim of his cowboy hat. The younger man's face paled visibly.

"Hearing things like that makes me real impatient," Ten said matter-of-factly. "When I get impatient, I get clumsy, and when I get clumsy, I break things. My friends are the same way, and I've got friends all over the Four Corners. So if you know any other pothunting cowards, pass the word. Starting now, my friends and I will be damned clumsy. Understand?"

Slowly Milt nodded.

Ten opened his hands and stepped back, his body both relaxed and perfectly balanced. "You're going to start thinking about this, and drinking, and pretty soon you'll be sure you can take me. So think on this. Next time you come after me, I'll strip you, pin a diaper on you, and walk you through town wearing a pink bonnet. Know something else? You won't have a mark on you, but you'll be marching double time just the same." Ten jerked his head toward the Rover. "Make sure I don't hear about you again, kid. I purely despise bullies."

Milt backed away from Ten and reached for the Rover's front door with more eagerness than grace. Ten watched. He was about to congratulate the two men in the Rover on their good sense in staying out of his way when he saw that the reason they had sidelined themselves wasn't good sense.

Diana had stepped down from the truck and was standing in the rain, sighting down a rifle she had braced across the hood of the truck.

Seven

With outward calm Diana watched the Range Rover slither and slide down the shale, retreating from September Canyon as quickly as the rain and rough terrain allowed.

"You can put it away now. They won't be back."

Ten's voice made Diana realize that she was still crouched over the rifle, sighting down its blue-steel barrel, her hands holding the weapon too tightly. She forced herself to take a deep breath and stand upright.

"May I?" Ten asked, holding out a hand for the rifle.

Diana gave the rifle to him and said faintly, "It will need cleaning. The rain is very... wet."

Ten didn't smile, simply nodded his head in agreement. "I'll take care of it."

"Thank you. It's been years since I cleaned a rifle. I've probably forgotten how."

"You sure didn't forget how to use one," Ten said as he checked the rifle over with a few swift movements. He noted approvingly that there was a round in the chamber. He removed the bullet and pocketed it. "Thanks."

Diana looked at him and blinked, trying to focus her thoughts.

"For aiming the rifle at them rather than at me," Ten explained, smiling slightly. "It's nice to know you think I'm one of the good guys."

"I—they—you didn't need me," she said, rubbing her hands together.

"Three against one? I needed all the help I could get."

Diana shook her head. "You could have made veal cutlets out of that pothunter before his friends could have taken a single step to stop you. Why didn't you?"

"Never did like veal cutlets," Ten said matter-of-factly, opening the truck door. "Get in, honey. It's wet out here."

"I'm serious," she said, climbing up into the dry cab. "Why did you hold back? You certainly didn't with Baker . . . did you?"

Ten went around the truck and got in behind the wheel. He sensed Diana's intent, watchful, rather wary eyes. Wondering if Diana were still afraid of him, Ten watched her from the corner of his eye as he began wiping down the rifle and shotgun. Despite the vague trembling of her hands and the paleness of her skin, he began to realize that she wasn't afraid of him; she was simply caught in the backlash of the adrenaline storm that had come from her brush with pothunters.

"Why?" Diana persisted, rubbing her arms as though she were cold.

"Baker is a brute who only understands brute force," Ten said finally. "If I had pulled my punches with him, he would have been back for more. That kid Milt was different. He's a swaggering bully. A coward. So I showed him what a candy ass he really is when it comes to fighting. He'll be a long time forgetting."

"Will he be back?"

"Doubt it." Ten turned around and locked the weapons back into the rack. "But if he does come back, he better pray Nevada isn't on guard."

"Nevada?"

"My kid brother. He would have gutted Milt and never looked back. Hard man, Nevada."

"And you aren't?"

Turning, looking at Diana over his shoulder, Ten smiled slowly. "Honey, haven't you figured it out yet? I'm so ten-derhearted a butterfly can walk roughshod all over me."

It was the second time in as many minutes that Ten had called Diana "honey." She knew she should object to the implied intimacy. At the very least she shouldn't encourage him by laughing at the ludicrous image of a butterfly stomping all over Ten's muscular body. So she tried very hard not to laugh, failed, and finally gave into the need, knowing that it was a release for all the emotions seething just beneath her control.

Ten listened, sensing the complex currents of Diana's emotions. He reached for the door before he looked over at her and nodded once, as though agreeing with himself.

"You'll do, Diana Saxton. You'll do just fine."

"For what?" she asked, startled.

"For whatever you want. You've got guts, lady. You'd go to war over a carton of Anasazi artifacts. You stand up for what you believe in. That's too damned rare these days."

Ten was out of the truck and closing the door behind him before Diana could put into words her first thought: she hadn't stood in the rain with an unfamiliar rifle in her hands to save a few artifacts from pothunters. It had been Ten she was worried about, one man against three.

I didn't need to worry. Ten is a one-man army. Cash was right. Someone taught Ten to play hardball. I wonder who, and where, and what it cost....

The truck's door opened. Ten set the closed carton of artifacts on the seat next to Diana, then swung into the cab with a lithe motion. His masculine grace fascinated her, as

did the fact that his rain-soaked shirt clung to every ridge
and swell of muscle, emphasizing the width of his shoulders and the strength of his back. If he had wanted to, he
could have overpowered her with terrible ease, for he was far
stronger than Steve had been; and in the end Steve had been
too strong for her.

Grimly Diana turned her thoughts away from a past that
was beyond her ability to change or forget. She could only
accept what had happened and renew her vow that she
would never again put herself in a position where a man
thought he had the right to take from her what she was un-
willing to give.

"Don't worry," Ten said.

"What?" Diana gave him a startled look, wondering if he
had read her mind.

"The artifacts are fine. Milt was an amateur when it came
to fighting, but he knew how to pack pots. Nothing was
lost."

"Just the history."

His hand on the key, Ten turned to look at Diana, not
understanding what she meant.

"The real value of the artifacts for an archaeologist comes
from seeing how they relate to each other in situ," she explained. "Unless these artifacts were photographed where
they were found, they don't have much to tell us now."

"To a scholar, maybe. But to me, just seeing the artifacts, seeing their shapes and designs, knowing they were
made by a people and a culture that lived and died and will
never be born again..." Ten shrugged. "I'd go to war to
save a piece of that. Hell, I have more than once."

Again, Ten had surprised Diana. She hadn't expected a
nonprofessional to understand the intellectual and emotional fascination of fragments from the past. His response
threw her off balance, leaving her teetering between her ingrained fear of men and her equally deep desire to be close
to the contradictory, complex man called Tennessee Blackthorn.

Ten eased the big truck down the slippery shoulder of shale and headed back for the big overhang that served as a base camp for the dig. By the time they had unloaded their gear, set up sleeping bags at the opposite ends of the overhang's broad base and changed into dry clothes behind the canvas privacy screen that had been erected for just such emergencies, the rain was becoming less a torrent.

Neither Diana nor Ten noticed the improving weather at first. They had gravitated toward the shard-sorting area that the graduate students had set up. Numbered cartons held remnants of pottery that had been taken from specific areas of the site. The shards themselves were also numbered according to the place where they had been unearthed. Whoever had the time or the desire was invited to try piecing together the three-dimensional puzzles before they were removed to the old ranch house.

Ten showed a marked flair for resurrecting whole artifacts from scattered, broken fragments. In fact, more than once Diana was astonished at the ease with which he reached into one carton, then another, and came out with interlocking shards. There was something uncanny about how pieces of history became whole in his hands. His concentration on the task made casual conversation unnecessary, which relieved Diana. Soon she was sorting shards, trying out pieces together, bending over Ten to reach into cartons, muttering phrases about gray ware with three black lines and an acute angle versus corrugated ware with a curve and a bite out of one side. Ten answered with similar phrases, handing her whatever he had that matched her description of missing shards.

After the first half hour Diana forgot that she was alone with a man in an isolated canyon. She forgot to be afraid that something she might say or do would trigger in Ten the certainty that she wanted him sexually despite whatever objections she might make to his advances. For the first time in years she enjoyed the company of a man as a person, another adult with whom she could be at ease.

When the rain finally stopped completely, Diana stood, stretched cramped leg muscles and went to the edge of the overhang to look out across the newly washed land. Although no ruins were visible from the overhang itself, excitement simmered suddenly in her blood. Hundreds of years ago the Anasazi had looked out on the same land, smelled the same scent of wet earth and piñon, seen the glittering beauty of sunlight captured in a billion drops of water clinging to needles and boughs and the sheer face of the cliff itself. For this instant she and the Anasazi were one.

That was what she wanted to capture in her illustrations—the continuity of life, of human experience, a continuity that existed through time regardless of the outward diversity of human cultures.

"I'm going to the site," Diana said, picking up her backpack.

Ten looked up from the potshards he was assembling. "I'll be along as soon as I get these numbered. Don't go up those ladders until they're dry. And stick to the part of the ruins that has a grid. Some of that rubble isn't stable, and some of the walls are worse."

"Don't worry. I'm not exploring anything alone. Too many of those ruins are traps waiting to be sprung. With the Anasazi, you never know when the ground is a ceiling covering a sunken kiva. I'll stay on the well-beaten paths until there are more people on site."

A long look assured Ten that Diana meant what she said. He nodded. "Thanks."

"For what?" she asked.

"Not getting your back up at my suggestions."

"I have nothing against common sense. Besides, you're the ramrod on this site. If I don't like your, er, 'suggestions,' that's my hard luck, right? You'll enforce your orders any way you have to."

Ten thought of putting it less bluntly, then shrugged. Diana was right, and it would save a lot of grief if she knew it.

"That's my job."

"I'll remember it."

What Diana said was the simple truth. She would remember. The thought of going against Ten's *suggestions* was frankly intimidating. He had the power to enforce his will and she knew it as well as he did. Better. She had been taught by her father and her fiancé just how little a woman's protests mattered to men whose physical superiority was a fact of life.

"If you hear the truck's horn beep three times, or three shots from the rifle," Ten said, "it means come back here on the double."

Diana nodded, checked her watch and said, "I'll be back before sundown."

"Damn straight you will be." He held two pieces of pottery up against the sunlight streaming into the overhang, frowned and set one piece aside before he said, "Only a fool or a pothunter would go feeling around in the ruins after dark."

Diana didn't bother to answer. Ten wasn't really listening anyway. He was holding another piece of pottery against the sunlight, visually comparing edges. They must have fit, because he grunted and wrote on the inside of both pieces. After they were cleaned they would be glued together, but the equipment for that operation was back at the old ranch house.

Beyond the overhang the land was damp and glistening from the recent rain. The short-lived waterfalls that had made lacy veils over the cliff faces were already diminishing to silver tendrils. Before she left the overhang, Diana glanced back at Ten, only to find him engrossed in his three-dimensional puzzle. She should have been relieved at the silent evidence that she didn't have to worry about fielding any unwanted advances from Ten. Quite obviously she wasn't the focus of his masculine attention.

But Diana wasn't relieved. She was a bit irked that he found it so easy to ignore her.

The realization disconcerted her, so she shoved the thought aside and concentrated on the increasingly rugged terrain as she began to climb from September Canyon's floor up to the base of the steep cliffs, following whatever truck tracks the rain hadn't washed away.

Summer thunder muttered through September Canyon, followed by a gust of rain-scented wind that made piñons moan. From the vantage point where the Rover had been parked, the ruins beckoned. Partial walls were scalloped raggedly by time and falling masonry. Some of the walls were barely ankle-high, others reached nearly twenty-five feet in height, broken only by the protruding cedar beams that had once supported floors. Cedar that was still protected by stone remained strong and hard. Exposed beams weathered with the excruciating slowness of rock itself.

Using a trick that an old archaeologist had taught her, Diana let her eyes become unfocused while she was looking at the ruins. Details blurred and faded, leaving only larger relationships visible, weights and masses, symmetry and balance, subtle uses of force and counterforce that had to be conceived in the human mind before they were built because they did not occur in nature. The multistoried wall with its T-shaped doors no longer looked like a chimney with bricks fallen out, nor did the roofless kivas look like too-wide wells. The relationship of roof to floor to ceiling, the geometries of shared-wall apartment living, became clearer to unfocused modern eyes.

The archaeologist who first examined September Canyon estimated that the canyon's alcove had held between nineteen and twenty-six rooms, including the ubiquitous circular kivas. The height of the building varied from less than four feet to three stories, depending on the height of the overhang itself.

The kivas were rather like basements set off from the larger grouping of rooms. The kivas' flat roofs were actually the floor of the town meeting area where children played and women ground corn, where dogs barked and chased foolish turkeys. The balcony of a third-story room was the ceiling of an adjacent two-story apartment. Cedar ladders reached to cistlike granaries built into lateral cracks too small to accommodate even a tiny room. And the Anasazi used rooms so tiny they were unthinkable to modern people, even taking into account the Anasazi's smaller stature.

Diana opened the outer pocket of her backpack and pulled out a lightweight, powerful pair of binoculars. As always, the patience of the Anasazi stonemasons fascinated her. Lacking metal of any kind, they shaped stone by using stone itself. Hand axes weighing several pounds were used to hammer rough squares or rectangles from shapeless slabs of rock. Then the imagined geometry was carefully tap-tap-tapped onto the rough block, thousands upon thousands of strokes, stone pecking at stone until the rock was of the proper shape and size.

The alcove's left side ended in sheer rock wall. A crack angled up the face of the cliff. At no point was the crack wider than a few inches, yet Diana could see places where natural foot- or handholds had been added. Every Anasazi who went up on the mesa to tend crops had to climb up the cliff with no more help than they could get out of the crack. The thought of making such a climb herself didn't appeal. The thought of children or old people making the climb in all kinds of weather was appalling, as was the thought of toddlers playing along the alcove's sheer drop.

Inevitably, people must have slipped and fallen. Even for an alcove that had a southern exposure protected from all but the worst storms, the kind of daily risking of life and limb represented by that trail seemed a terrible price to pay.

Diana lowered the glasses, looked at the ruins with her unaided eyes and frowned. The angle wasn't quite right for what she wanted to accomplish. Farther up the canyon, where the rubble slopes rose to the point that an agile climber could reach the ruins without a ladder, the angle would be no better. What she needed was a good spot from

which to sketch an overview of the countryside with an in-
set detailing the structure and placement of the ruins themselves. The surrounding country could be sketched almost
anytime. The ruins, however, were best sketched in slanting, late-afternoon light, when all the irregularities and angles of masonry leaped into high relief. That "sweet light"
was rapidly developing as the day advanced.

With measuring eyes, Diana scanned her surroundings
before she decided to sketch from the opposite side of the
canyon. She shrugged her backpack into a more comfortable position and set off. The rains had been light enough
that September Creek was a ribbon she could jump over
without much danger of getting her feet wet. She worked her
way up the canyon until she was half a mile above the ruins
on the opposite side. Only then did she climb up the talus
slope at the base of the canyon's stone walls.

When Diana could climb no higher without encounter-
ing solid rock, she began scrambling parallel to the base of
the cliff that formed the canyon wall. Every few minutes she
paused to look at the ruins across the canyon, checking the
changing angles until she found one she liked. Her strategy
meant a hard scramble across the debris slope at the base of
the canyon's wall, but she had made similar scrambles at
other sites in order to find just the right place to sit and
sketch.

Finally Diana stopped at the top of a particularly steep
scramble where a section of the sandstone cliff had sloughed
away, burying everything beneath in chunks of stone as big
as a truck. She wiped her forehead, checked the angle of the
ruins and sighed.

"Close, but not good enough." She looked at the debris
slope ahead, then at the ruins again. "Just a bit farther. I
hope."

Climbing carefully, scrambling much of the time, her
hands and clothes redolent of the evergreens she had
grabbed to pull herself along the steepest parts, Diana
moved along the cliff base. Suddenly she saw a curving

something on the ground that was the wrong color and shape to be a stone. She walked eagerly forward, bending to pick up the potshard, which glowed an unusual red in the slanting sunlight. No sooner had her fingers curled around the shard than the ground gave way beneath her feet, sending her down in a torrent of dirt and stone.

Clutching at air, screaming, she plunged into darkness, and the name she screamed was Ten's.

Eight

Ten was running before Diana's scream ended abruptly, leaving silence and echoes in its wake. He raced away from the ruins at full speed, not needing to follow Diana's tracks in order to find her. In the first instant of her scream he had seen her red windbreaker vividly against the creamy wall of stone on the opposite side of the canyon.

And then the red had vanished.

"Diana! *Diana!*"

No one answered Ten's shout. He saved his breath for running across the canyon bottom and scrambling up the steep slope. As soon as he saw the black shadow of the new hole in the ground he realized what had happened. Diana had stepped onto the concealed roof of a kiva and it had given way beneath her weight. Some of the kivas were only a few feet deep. Others were deeper than a man was tall. He was afraid that Diana had found one of the deep ones.

Moving slowly, ready to throw himself aside at the first hint of uncertain footing, Ten crept close to the hole that had appeared in the rubble slope.

"Diana, can you hear me?"

A sound that might have been his name came from the hole.

"Don't move," he said. "If you've hurt your spine, you could make it worse by thrashing around. I'll get to you as soon as I can."

This time Ten was certain that the sound Diana made was his name.

"Just lie still and close your eyes in case I knock some more dirt loose."

On his stomach, Ten inched closer to the hole. At the far side he saw stubs of the cedar poles that had once supported a segment of the ceiling. In front of him was an open slot where Diana had gone through about a third of the way across the circular ceiling. Parallel, intact cedar poles crossed the opening Diana had accidentally made.

Ten pulled himself to the edge of the hole and peered over. Eight feet down Diana lay half-buried in rubble, surrounded by a circle of carefully fitted masonry wall.

"I'm coming down now. Just lie still."

Ten tested the cedar poles as best he could. They held. Bracing himself between two poles, praying that the tough cedar would hold under his weight, he slipped through the ceiling and landed lightly on his feet next to Diana. Instinctively she tried to sit up.

"Don't move!"

"Can't—breathe."

The ragged gasps told Ten that she was breathing more effectively than she knew.

"It's all right. You had the wind knocked out by the fall, but you're getting it back now. Does any place in particular hurt?"

"No—"

Ten went down on his knees next to Diana's head. Her eyes went wide and she dragged raggedly at air when he reached for her.

"Easy now, honey," he murmured. "I've got to check you for injuries. Just lie still. I won't hurt you. Be still now. It's all right."

Dazed, helpless, Diana fought her fear and held on to the black velvet of Ten's voice, remembering the moments when he had soothed the panicked horse and held the injured kitten so gently. It was the same now, hands both strong and gentle probing her scalp, her neck, her shoulders, his voice soothing, directing, explaining; and all the while debris was being pushed away, revealing more of her body to Ten's thorough touch, his hands moving over her with an intimacy that she had never willingly allowed any man. All that kept her from panicking was the realization that his hands were as impersonal as they were careful.

"I can't feel anything broken and you didn't flinch anywhere when I touched you," Ten said finally. "Any numb spots?"

"No—I felt—" Diana sucked in air as much from the emotional shock of being touched as from the force of her recent fall. "Everywhere—you touched—I felt."

"Good. Wiggle your fingers and toes for me."

Diana did.

"Hurt?"

"No."

"I'm going to check your neck again. If it hurts, even a little, you tell me quick."

Long fingers eased once more around Diana's neck, working their way through her hair, taking the weight of her head so slowly that she hardly realized when she was no longer supporting it herself.

"Hurt?"

"N-no."

Ten's fingers spread, surrounding the back of her head, and his thumbs glided gently over the line of her jaw.

Diana's breath came in and stayed, trapped by the sensations shivering through her. So slowly that she realized it only after the fact, Ten began to turn her head to the right.

"Hurt?"

She tried to speak, couldn't, and shook her head instead. His smile flashed for an instant in the gloom.

"If shaking your head didn't hurt, you're okay. Let's see how you do sitting up. We'll take it slow. If your back hurts at any time, tell me. Ready?"

Diana didn't need Ten's assistance to sit up, but she got it anyway. His left arm was a hard, warm, resilient bar supporting her shoulders and his right arm rested across her chest, preventing her from pitching forward if she fainted, which she nearly did at the pressure of his forearm across her suddenly sensitive breasts.

"I'm fine," Diana said in a breathless rush.

"So far so good," agreed Ten. "Dizzy?"

She was, but it had nothing to do with her recent fall and everything to do with the powerful man kneeling next to her in the shadows of an ancient kiva, his arms supporting her, his face so close to hers that she tasted his very breath.

"I'm not—dizzy."

"Good. We'll just sit here for a minute and make sure."

While Ten studied the broken ceiling overhead, Diana studied him. For the first time she was struck by how truly handsome he was with his black, slightly curling hair, broad forehead, widely spaced gray eyes, thick lashes, straight nose, high cheekbones and a beard shadow that heightened the intensely male line of his jaw.

It was more than the regularity of Ten's features that appealed to Diana so vividly at the moment; it was the certainty that his abundant masculine strength wasn't going to be used against her. The relief was dizzying, telling her how much of her energy had been locked up in controlling her fear of men.

Then Diana realized that Ten was looking at her. The clarity of his gray eyes was extraordinary. The clean curves and angles of his mouth made her think of touching him, of finding out if his lips tasted as good as his breath.

"Are you all right?" he asked. "You look a little dazed."

"I am." Diana took a ragged breath, then another. "Having the world jerked out from under your feet does that."

Ten's smile flashed again. "Yeah, I guess so. Ready to try standing up?"

"Um."

"We'll take it nice and easy. Just onto your knees at first. Here we go."

With an ease that would have terrified Diana only yesterday, Ten lifted her into a kneeling position. His eyes measured her response, his hands felt the continued coordination of her body as she took her own weight on her knees, and he nodded.

"Ready to try standing? I don't want to rush you, but I'll feel a lot better once we're out of this kiva."

For the first time the nature of her surroundings sank into Diana.

"A kiva! I fell through the ceiling of a kiva?"

"You sure did, honey."

"We have to mark the site and be careful not to do any more damage and—"

"First," Ten interrupted smoothly, "we have to get the hell out of here. It's dangerous."

The voice was still black velvet, but there was the cool reality of steel beneath.

"Ramrod," she breathed.

"Ready?" was all Ten said.

Ready or not, Diana was on her feet a few seconds later, put there by Ten's easy strength. She braced herself momentarily on his hard forearms, feeling the vital heat of his body radiating through cloth. She snatched back her hands as though she had been burned.

"I'm fine," she said quickly. "Really. I can stand alone."

Ten heard Diana's uneasiness in the sudden tumble of words and released her. He didn't step back, for he wanted to be able to catch her if her knees gave way.

"No dizziness?" he asked.

There was, but it came from Ten's closeness rather than from any injury she might have received in the fall. Diana had no intention of saying anything about that fact, however.

"No," she said firmly. "I'm not dizzy."

"Sure?"

"Where have I heard that question before?"

A smile flashed in the gloom, Ten's smile, warm against the hard lines of his face.

"Feeling feisty, are you?" he asked.

Diana looked away from Ten, afraid her approval of him would be much too clear. She didn't want that. She didn't want to give him any reason to expect anything from her as a woman. With narrowed eyes, she examined the hole in the ceiling that was their only exit from the kiva. If she stretched up all the way on her tiptoes she might be able to brush her fingertips close to a cedar beam. And then again, she might not.

"Actually, I'm feeling rather intimidated," she admitted. "Some women would be able to get out of this hole alone, but not me. In gym classes I was a total disaster at chinning myself on the high bar."

Ten measured the distance to the ceiling and the cedar beams. "No problem. God made men with that in mind."

"He did?"

Ten nodded and kicked aside a bit of loose rubble, giving himself stable footing beneath the hole. He braced his legs and held out his arms to Diana.

"Okay, honey. Up you go."

She looked at him as though he had just suggested that she teleport herself out of the hole.

"Don't worry, I won't drop you," Ten said. "I handle heavier things every day. I'll lift you up. You balance yourself on the cedar poles until you can scramble from my shoulders to the ground."

"What about you?"

"That's where God's design comes in. He made men stronger than women." The smile faded, leaving only the hard male lines of Ten's face. "It's all right, Diana. I won't hurt you. Trust me."

"I—" Her voice broke. She swallowed and forced herself to take the two steps toward Ten. "I'll—try. What do I have to do?"

"First, put your hands on my shoulders."

For a few moments Diana was afraid she wouldn't be able to force herself to do it. Silently, fiercely, she closed her eyes and fought old fears.

Ten watched with narrowed eyes, feeling Diana's fear as clearly as he had the soft feminine curves of her body while he checked her for injury.

"Diana. Put your hands on my shoulders."

Her eyelids snapped open. Gone was the velvet reassurance of Ten's voice. In its place was a steel reality: she could help Ten get her out of the kiva or she could fight him; either way, she was going up through that hole in the ceiling. Diana didn't know how he would manage the feat without her cooperation, but she had no doubt that he would.

Diana lifted her hands to Ten's shoulders. She knew he felt her trembling but was unable to stop it.

"Are you afraid of falling again?" he asked.

"I—"

Her hands clenched around the hard resilience of Ten's shoulder muscles. He was so strong. Much too strong. She was as helpless as a kitten against his power.

Remember that tiger-striped kitten cuddled in Ten's hands. The kitten was relaxed, purring, trusting. Ten didn't hurt that sick kitten. He won't hurt me.

"What d-do you want me to do?" Diana asked, forgetting everything except the need to hold on to her belief that Ten wouldn't hurt her.

"Brace yourself on my shoulders. I'm going to lift you until you can grab a cedar pole. Use it to help you kneel on my shoulders, then stand on them. From there you should be able to get out of the kiva without much problem. Okay?"

She nodded, gripped his shoulders more tightly and braced herself for whatever might come.

"Not yet," Ten said, stroking Diana's back slowly. "You're shaking too much. Slow down, honey. You're all right."

"Being p-petted is just going to make me m-more nervous."

One black eyebrow lifted, but Ten said nothing except "Hang on. Here we go. And keep your back straight."

Diana didn't understand the last instruction until she felt the brush of Ten's body over hers as he bent his knees, wrapped his arms around her thighs and straightened, lifting her within reach of the cedar poles. He need not have worried about her back being straight—her whole body went rigid at the intimacy of his powerful arms locked around her thighs and his head pressed against her abdomen.

"Ten!"

"It's okay, honey. I've got you."

That's the whole problem! But Diana had just enough control left not to blurt out her thought.

"Can you grab one of the poles yet?" Ten asked.

Diana pulled her scattering thoughts together, lifted one hand from the corded muscle of Ten's shoulder and grabbed a cedar pole. It was as hard as Ten but not nearly so warm.

"Got it," she said breathlessly.

"Good. Now grab the other pole."

A few seconds, then, "Okay. I've got that one, too."

"Hang on."

Ten moved so quickly that Diana was never sure how he had managed it, but within seconds she was kneeling on his shoulders, using her grip on the poles for balance. His hands on her hips were holding her firmly and his face was—

Don't think about it or you'll fall.

"Steady, honey," Ten said in a muffled voice.

"Easy for you to say," Diana muttered through clenched teeth.

He laughed softly.

She felt the intimate heat of his breath.

"Oh, God."

"What's wrong?" Ten asked. "Is one of the beams rotten?"

Diana didn't answer. She pulled herself up and out of the kiva before she had a chance to question the shivering sensations that cascaded throughout her body. She scrambled back from the edge and sat hugging herself, feeling flushed in the most unnerving places.

"Everything okay?" Ten called.

"Yes. No. I—" She clenched her teeth. "Fine. Just fine."

"Get back. I'm coming out."

Diana scooted back away from the hole, wondering how Ten was planning to get out. A few seconds later, two hands closed around a cedar pole. With a grace that startled her, Ten chinned himself, held himself one-handed while he grabbed the second pole with his other hand, swung his legs up and levered himself out of the hole with the ease of a gymnast at work on a set of parallel bars.

"Where did you learn how to do that?" Diana asked.

"Same place I learned to patch up kittens."

"Where was that?"

"Long ago, far away, in another country."

"But where?" she persisted. "Why?"

"Commando training."

Diana opened her mouth but no words came out.

Commando training.

Ten held out his hand to help Diana to her feet. "Let's go, honey. The sun will be setting soon."

A wild glance at the sky told Diana that Ten was right. The sun would soon slip beneath the horizon, leaving her alone in the dark at the ends of the earth with a man who was not only far more powerful than she but who was trained to be a killer, as well.

"You sure you're all right?" Ten asked, sitting on his heels next to Diana. "If you can't walk, I'll carry you."

She flinched away from him before she could grab her unraveling courage in both hands. She gave Ten a searching look but saw no triumph in his expression, no malice, no brute hunger, nothing but polite concern for her welfare.

"I can—" Diana's voice broke. She swallowed. "I can walk."

Ten started to reach for her, saw her flinch away and dropped his hand. He stood and moved a pace back from her.

"Get up. We'll drive back to the ranch after we eat," he said matter-of-factly.

"What? Why?"

"You know why," Ten said, turning away from Diana. "Every time I come close to you, you cringe. You'll feel more at ease with one of the other men."

"No!"

The stark emotion in Diana's voice stopped Ten. He looked back at her.

"Please stay," she said quickly. "I trust you more than I've trusted any man since—since I—since he—Ten, please! It's nothing you've done. It's nothing personal. Please believe me."

"It's hard to," he said bluntly.

"Then believe this. You're the first man who's touched me in any way for years and it scares me to death because I'm not scared and you're so damned *male*."

Ten's eyes narrowed. "You're not making much sense."

"I know. I'll get better. I promise."

For a moment Ten looked at Diana. Then he nodded slowly and held out his hand. If she stretched she could take it and help herself up. She looked at the lean hand and remembered the strength and lethal skill of the man behind it.

Then Diana took Ten's hand in both of hers and pulled herself to her feet.

Nine

While the night wind blew outside, Diana sat in the old ranch house, staring at a potshard in her palm, remembering the incident two weeks ago when Ten had dropped down into the darkness beside her and lifted her to the solid ground above. The tactile memories had haunted her . . . his hands searching carefully over her body, his easy strength when he lifted her, his face pressed so intimately against her while she climbed back into sunshine.

Shivering, remembering, Diana saw nothing of the shard in her palm. The memories resonated in her body as much as in her mind, sending sensations rippling through her, heat and cold, uneasiness and curiosity, a strange hunger to touch Ten in return, to know his masculine textures as well as he knew her feminine ones.

I'm going crazy.

Once more Diana tried to concentrate on the shard lying across her palm, but all she could think about was the instant when she had taken Ten's hand between her own and pulled herself to her feet. She thought she had felt his fingers caressing her in the very act of releasing her, but the touch had stopped before she could be certain.

And since then Ten had been the heart, soul and body of asexual politeness. At the site he treated her with the casual camaraderie of an older brother. It was the same at the ranch. At night they sorted shards together, spoke in broken phrases about missing angles and notched curves, discussed the weather or the ranch or the progress of the dig in slightly more complete sentences—and he never touched her, even when he seated her at the dinner table or passed a box of shards to her or looked over her shoulder to offer advice about a missing piece of a pot. He had every excuse to crowd her personal space from time to time, but he didn't.

For the first few days Ten's distance had reassured Diana. Then it had piqued her interest. By the fourteenth day it outright annoyed her.

You'd think I didn't shower often enough.

"Did you say something?" Ten asked from across the table.

Appalled, Diana realized that she had muttered her thought aloud.

"Nothing," she said quickly.

A few moments later she put the shard aside and stood up, feeling restless. As it often did, her glance strayed to the man who had shared so many days and evenings and nights with her.

The nights were perfectly proper, of course. Some outlaw. The Rocking M's ramrod is nothing if not proper.

Broodingly Diana watched Ten's long fingers turning potshards over and over, handling the fragile pottery deftly, running his fingertips over the edges as though to learn the tiniest contours by touch alone. She did the same thing when she worked, a kind of tactile exploration that was as much a part of her nature as her expressive eyes and her fear of men.

But she no longer feared men. At least, not all men. Luke still startled her from time to time with his sheer size, yet she had no doubt that Carla was perfectly safe with her chosen man, as was little Logan with his father, a father chosen by fate rather than by the baby. Not all children were that lucky in their parents. Diana hadn't been. Nor were all wives as fortunate in their husbands. Diana's mother certainly had not been safe or cherished with her man.

Restlessly, Diana ran her fingertips over the tabletop, feeling the grit that rubbed off the shards no matter how carefully they were handled. She smoothed her fingers over the table's surface again and again, watching Ten's hands, fascinated by their combination of power and precision.

What would it feel like to be touched with such care?

The glittering sensation that shivered through Diana at her silent question made her feel almost weak. She wanted to be touched by Ten, but it was impossible. He was a man. He would want more than touching, gentleness, cherishing, holding.

With a small sound Diana looked away from Ten. She didn't notice the sudden intensity in his eyes as he watched her over the pot he was assembling from ancient shards.

"Mmrreeow?"

The polite query was followed by another, less polite one. Diana hurried to the window, grateful to have a distraction from her unexpected, unnerving attraction to Ten.

"Hello, you old reprobate," she said, opening the window and holding out her arms.

On a gust of air, the tiger-striped cat flowed into Diana's arms. Pounce's fur smelled cool, fresh, washed by the clean wind. Smiling, rubbing her face against the cat's sleek head, she settled back into her chair. Pounce's rumbling, vibrating approval rippled out, blending with the fitful sound of the wind.

"King of the Rocking M, aren't you?" she asked, smiling. "Think you can trade a few dead mice for some time in my lap, hmm?"

Ten looked up again. Diana was kneading gently down the cat's big back, rubbing her cheek against Pounce's head while he rubbed his head against her in turn. The old mouser's purring was like continuous, distant thunder, but it was Diana's clear enjoyment of the cat's textures and responses that brought every one of Ten's masculine senses alert. He had kept his distance from her very carefully since the first day at the site; he would never forget the raw terror that he had seen in her eyes the first time he had reached for her in the gloom of the ancient kiva.

No matter how carefully Diana tried to conceal it, Ten sensed that she was still afraid of him. Perhaps it was because the first time she had seen him, he was the victor in a brief, brutal fight. Perhaps it was the way he had handled the pothunters. Perhaps it was his commando training. Perhaps it was simply himself, Tennessee Blackthorn, a man who never had worn well on women—and vice versa. An outlaw, not a lover or a husband.

Pounce purred loudly from Diana's lap, proclaiming his satisfaction with life, himself and the woman who was stroking his sleek body.

"If I thought you'd give me a rubdown like that, I'd go out and catch mice, too."

Diana gave Ten a startled look.

"Don't know that I'd eat them, though," Ten added blandly, measuring a shard against the bright lamplight. "A man has to draw the line somewhere."

Uncertainly Diana laughed. The idea of Ten purring beneath her hands made odd sensations shiver through her. Surely he was joking. But if he weren't . . .

Shadows of old fear rose in Diana. When she spoke her voice was tight and the words came out in a torrent, for she was afraid of being interrupted before she got everything said that had to be said.

"You'd be better off eating Carla's wonderful chicken than trading dead mice for a pat from me. I'm not the sensual type. Sex is for men, not women. In the jargon, I'm frigid, if frigid defines a woman who can live very well without sex."

Ten looked up sharply, caught as much by the palpable resonances of fear in Diana's voice as he was by her words. He started to speak but she was still talking, words spilling out like water from a river finally freed of its lid of winter ice.

"A man must have thought up the word *frigid,*" Diana continued quickly. "A woman would just say she isn't a masochist, that she feels no need of pain, self-inflicted or otherwise. But no matter what label you put on it—and me—the result is the same. Thanks but no thanks."

The words echoed in the quiet room. Their defensiveness made Diana cringe inside, but she wouldn't have taken back a single blunt syllable. Ten had to know.

"I don't recall asking you for sex," Ten said.

For a long minute Diana's hands kneaded through Pounce's fur, soothing the cat and herself at the same time, drawing forth a lifting and falling rumble of purrs.

"No, you haven't," she said finally, sighing, feeling herself relax now that the worst of it was over. Ten knew. He could never accuse her now. "But I've learned the hard way that it's better to be honest than to be quiet and then be accused of being a tease."

"Don't worry, Diana. Like the moon goddess you're named after, you've got No Trespassing signs posted all over you. Any man who doesn't see them would have to be as blind as you are."

"What?"

Ten looked up from the shards he had assembled. "You're stone-blind to your own basic nature. You're not frigid. You have a rare sensuality. You drink storm winds and nuzzle Logan's tiny hands and touch pieces of pottery with fingertips that are so sensitive you don't even have to look to tell what kind of edge there is. You rub that old tomcat until he's a vibrating pudding of pleasure, and you enjoy it just as much as he does. That's all sensuality is—

taking pleasure in your own senses. And sex, good sex, is the most pleasure your senses can stand.''

Diana sat transfixed, caught within the diamond clarity of Ten's eyes watching her, the black velvet certainty of his voice caressing her. Then he looked back to the shards, releasing her.

"Did a new box come in from the site?" Ten asked in a calm voice, as though they had never discussed anything more personal than potshards. "I've been waiting for one from 10-B. I think part of this red pot might have washed down to that spot on the grid. A long time ago, of course."

Her mind in turmoil, Diana grabbed the question, grateful to have something neutral to talk about. "Yes, it's over there. I'll get it."

If Ten noticed the rapid-fire style of Diana's speech, he didn't comment.

Releasing a reluctant Pounce, Diana went to the corner of the room where recently cleaned, permanently numbered shards were stored in hope of future assembling. The carton collected from 10-B on the site grid was on top of the pile. She brought the box to the long table where Ten worked by the light of a powerful gooseneck lamp.

"Thanks," he said absently. "I don't suppose there's a piece lying around on top with two obtuse angles and a ragged bite out of the third side?"

"Gray? Corrugated? Black on white?"

"Red."

"Really?" she asked, excited. Redware was the most unusual of all the Anasazi pottery. It also came from the last period when they inhabited the northern reaches of their homeland. "Do you think we have enough shards to make a whole pot?"

Ten made a rumble that sounded suspiciously like Pounce at his most satisfied. He leaned over, pulled a large carton from beneath the table and folded back the flaps. With gentle care he lifted pieces of an ancient bowl onto the table. The background color of the pot was brick red. Designs in white and black covered the surface, careful geometrics that spoke of a painstaking artist working patiently over the pot.

A feeling of awe expanded through Diana as she saw the pot lying half-mended on the table. Ten had been as patient and painstaking as the original potter; the fine lines where he had glued shards together were almost invisible.

"You never did tell me why this kind of pot is so rare," Ten said, turning aside to the carton of unmatched shards.

"Polychrome pots are usually found south of here," Diana said absently. Her hands closed delicately around the base and a curving side of the red pot. "Either the potter was an immigrant or the pot was a piece of trade goods. But this pot, plus the surface and regular shape of the sandstone masonry in September Canyon, make it certain that the site is from the Pueblo III period of the Anasazi. Or nearly certain. Since we don't have a time machine, we'll never be one hundred percent positive that we have the true story."

"We know the most important thing."

Diana looked up from the fragment of the past held between her hands.

"They were people like us," Ten said simply. "They built, laughed, wept, fought, raised children and died. Most of all, they knew fear."

"Actually," Diana said, frowning over the box of shards, "the most recent theory states that the Anasazi moved into their cliff houses for reasons other than fear."

Ten's left eyebrow arched skeptically. "They just liked the view halfway up the cliff, huh?"

"Um, no one said anything about that. The theory just states that we were premature in attributing a fortress mentality to the Anasazi. They could just have been preserving the top of the mesa for crops and didn't build on the canyon bottom because of floods. That left the cliffs themselves for housing."

Ten grunted. "What did the professorial types say about the signal towers on top of Mesa Verde? They were used to pass the news of births, right?"

Diana gave Ten a sideways look, but he appeared to be engrossed in the red potshards she was finding and carefully placing in front of him. Already he had found two to glue together and was positioning a third.

"The towers could have been used to welcome visitors," Diana said neutrally, "or to show the way up onto the mesa for people who were from other areas."

"People from other areas tend to be strangers and strangers tend to be unfriendly."

"Perhaps the Anasazi believed that strangers were simply friends they hadn't met yet."

"That would certainly explain how the Anasazi died out so fast," Ten said sardonically.

"In some academic circles, your point of view would be considered philosophically and politically retrograde," Diana said without heat. One of the most pleasurable things about her time with Ten was the discovery of his agile, wide-ranging mind. She had come to look forward to the hours spent sorting shards and talking about the Anasazi almost as much as she enjoyed working on the site itself. "Here's the shard that goes in the middle."

"Thanks," Ten said. "Hang on to it until the glue dries on these two. Whatever made the professors give up on good old common sense to explain the Anasazi cliff dwellings?"

"Such as?"

"Birds don't fly because they like the view up there. Birds fly because cats can't."

Diana smiled. "Don't tell Pounce."

"I don't have to. He figured that one out all by himself, which is more than I can say for whoever dreamed up that New Age fertilizer about cliff houses being invented for any reason other than self-defense. In a word, fear."

YOURS

We'd like to send you four free Silhouette novels, worth $10.00, to introduce you to the benefits of the Silhouette Reader Service™. We hope your free books will convince you to subscribe, but that's up to you. Accepting them places you under no obligation to buy anything, but we hope you'll want to continue your membership in the Reader Service.

So unless we hear from you, once a month we'll send you six additional Silhouette Desire™ novels to read and enjoy. If you choose to keep them, you'll pay just $2.24* each—a saving of 26¢ off the cover price—plus only 69¢ postage and handling for the entire shipment! And you may cancel at any time, for any reason, just by sending us a note or a shipping statement marked "cancel", or by returning any shipment of books to us at our cost. Either way, the free books and gifts are yours to keep!

ALSO FREE!
VICTORIAN PICTURE FRAME

This lovely Victorian pewter-finish miniature is perfect for displaying a treasured photograph—and it's yours *absolutely free*—when you accept our no-risk offer.

Perfect for a treasured Photograph

Plus a FREE mystery Gift! follow instructions at right.

SILHOUETTE DESIRE® NOVELS
FREE!

 Silhouette Reader Service™

```
AFFIX
FOUR FREE BOOKS
STICKER HERE
```

YES, send me my four free books and gifts as explained on the opposite page. I have affixed my "free books" sticker above and my two "free gift" stickers below. I understand that accepting these books and gifts places me under no obligation ever to buy any books; I may cancel at anytime, for any reason, and the free books and gifts will be mine to keep!

326 CIS ACFY (C-SIL-D-02/91)

NAME _____

(PLEASE PRINT)

ADDRESS _____ APT. _____

CITY _____

PROV. _____ POSTAL CODE _____

```
AFFIX FREE
VICTORIAN
PICTURE
FRAME
STICKER HERE
```

```
AFFIX FREE
MYSTERY GIFT
STICKER HERE
```

PRINTED IN U.S.A.

WE EVEN PROVIDE FREE POSTAGE!

It costs you *nothing* to send for your free books — we've paid the postage on the attached reply card. And we'll pick up the postage on your shipment of free books and gifts!

**Business
Reply Mail**

No Postage Stamp
Necessary if Mailed
in Canada

Postage will be paid by

Silhouette Reader Service™

P.O. Box 609
Fort Erie, Ontario
L2A 9Z9

Canada Post
Postes Canada
125

"Logical, but it doesn't explain why there was no increase in burials about the time the Anasazi abandoned the mesa tops and took up living in the cliffs."

"Burials?"

"Self-defense indicates war," Diana explained. "War indicates wounding and death. Death—"

"Leads to burials," Ten interrupted.

"Right. Even around the time the Anasazi disappeared altogether, there was no increase in burials. Therefore, the theory that hostile tribes forced the Anasazi into cliff houses has a big flaw. No extra deaths, no war. Simple."

"More like simpleminded. Those theorists ought to pull their heads out of their, er, books and have a reality check."

"What do you mean?"

"Only winners bury their dead."

The flatness in Ten's voice made a chill move over Diana's skin.

"You sound very certain," she said.

"I've been there. That's as certain as it gets."

"There?"

"On the losing side. It hasn't changed all that much over the centuries. I doubt that it ever will. Pain, fear, death and not enough people left to mourn or bury the dead. But there are always enough vultures."

Ten's narrowed eyes were like splinters of clear glass. Diana could not bear to look at them and think of what they had seen.

He turned and searched through the box of potshards. When he looked up again, his expression was once more relaxed.

"In any case," Ten continued, "anybody who's read a little biology could tell your fancy theorists that building Stone Age apartment houses halfway up sheer cliffs took an immense amount of time and energy, which meant that the need driving the society also had to be immense. Survival is the most likely explanation, and the only animal that

threatens man's survival is man himself." Ten smiled grimly.
"That hasn't changed, either."

"Fear."

"Don't knock it. No animal would survive without it,
including man." Ten held a shard up to the light, shrugged
and tried it anyway. It fit. "Maybe the Anasazi were no
longer actively involved in war. Maybe they just feared it to
the point that they retreated to a hole in the cliffs and pulled
the hole in after them." Ten looked up. "You can understand that kind of fear, can't you? It's what drew you to the
Anasazi in the first place. Like you, they built a shell around
themselves to wall out the world. And then they began to
shrink and die inside that shell."

Diana concentrated on two shards that had no chance of
fitting.

Ten waited a few moments, sighed and continued. "When
you retreat to a stone cliff that's accessible only by one or
two eyelash trails that a nine-year-old with a sharp stick
could defend, it's probably because you don't have much
more than nine-year-olds left to defend the village."

"But there's no hard evidence of repeated encounters with
a warlike tribe," she said coolly.

"Isn't there? What does Anasazi mean?"

"It's a Navajo word meaning Ancient Ones, or Those
Who Came Before."

Ten smiled thinly. "It also means Enemy Ancestor." He
picked up an oddly shaped shard and stared at it without
really seeing it. "I suspect that at the end of a long, hard
period, during which they'd had to cope with war or
drought or disease or all three, a kind of madness overtook
the northern Anasazi."

The quality of Ten's voice, rippling with something un-
spoken, caught Diana's attention.

"What do you mean?"

"I think a dark kind of shaman cult overtook them, using up everything the society had and demanding even more.
Maybe the fears the shaman cult played on had some basis

in reality, or maybe they lived only in the Anasazi's own nightmares.'' Ten shook his head. ''Either way, fear ruled the society. The people retreated to the most impossible places they could reach and walled themselves in with rooms and held ceremonies in buried kivas. When they ran out of space in the alcoves, they built bigger and bigger kivas along the base of the cliff.''

Ten's voice shifted, becoming subtly different, more resonant yet softer.

''Their rituals became more and more elaborate,'' he continued quietly, ''more demanding of the people's mental and physical resources. Darker. It's possible for a culture to exist like that, but not for long. It goes against the deepest grain of survival to huddle in a stone crypt.''

''Is that what you think happened? The Anasazi died in the city crypts they built for themselves?''

''Some did. Some escaped.''

The odd timbre of Ten's voice made the hair on Diana's scalp stir in primal response, the same stirring she had felt with Ten once before, when she had stood on a desolate mesa top and felt centuries like cards being shuffled, revealing glimpses of a time when reality had been very different, and so had she and Ten.

''How did they escape?'' Diana asked, her voice strange even to her own ears.

For a long time there was only silence punctuated by the sounds of the wind sweeping over the ancient land. Just when Diana had decided that Ten wasn't going to say any more, he began speaking again.

''Another shaman came down from the north, an outlaw shaman with a vision that swept through the Anasazi, a vision that spoke of light as well as darkness, life as well as death.'' Ten looked up suddenly, catching and holding Diana with eyes as clear as rain. ''The Anasazi who believed the outlaw shaman climbed down out of their beautiful, dangerous, futile cliff cities and never went back again.''

Ten

Luke leaned toward little Logan, smiling, speaking in a deep, gentle voice to the baby who studied him so intently.

"Definitely your eyes, Carla," Luke said, running his fingertip over his wife's cheek.

"The mouth is yours, though," she said, smoothing her cheek over his hand.

"We're in trouble then. He'll have half the state mad at him as soon as he learns to talk."

Carla laughed softly, brushed her lips over Luke's palm and settled back against his chest. The nursing shawl slipped to one side, revealing the milk-swollen curve of her breast. With a slow caress Luke adjusted the shawl, then resumed the gentle back-and-forth motion of the big rocking chair he had made before Logan had been born.

Despite its size, the chair was still a snug fit for the three of them—Logan, Carla and Luke—but no one had any intention of giving it up for the couch. The quiet evenings when Carla nursed the baby while sitting in Luke's lap had become the highlight of the day for everyone involved.

"Hi," Carla said, looking up as Diana came from the kitchen into the living room. "Ten was asking about you a few minutes ago. Something about a box from 11-C?"

"More red shards. He hopes. He has this theory about where the rest of the red pot is. So far he has been right."

A night of broken sleep and restless dreams had convinced Diana that Ten had been right about more than the pot, but she didn't know how to reopen the subject with him, any more than she had known how to respond last night, when he had spoken about fear and the Anasazi and one Diana Saxton. Instead of speaking then, she had handed him another shard and the conversation had disintegrated into elliptical phrases describing pieces of broken pots.

"Is Ten in the bunkhouse?" Diana asked.

"He's in the barn checking on a lame horse."

Diana hid her feeling of disappointment. Whether in September Canyon or at the ranch headquarters, she looked forward to the evenings with Ten despite the tension that came from her increasing awareness of him as a man. She noticed him in ways that she had never noticed any man at all. The dense black of his eyelashes, the equally dense beard shadow that lay beneath his skin no matter how recently he had shaved, the springy thatch of hair that showed beneath his open collar, the endless flex and play of muscles beneath his skin, the easy stride of a man who was at home in and confident of his body.

But most of all, Diana noticed the frank masculinity of Ten, the male sensuality that was both subtle and pervasive. It compelled her senses in the same way that his intelligence compelled her mind.

"If you see Ten," Diana said to Carla, "tell him I've cleaned the calcium deposits from the 11-C shards, given them permanent labels, and they're ready for his magic touch."

"Sure. Want to stay for pie? We're having some as soon as we put our greedy son to bed."

"No thanks. Your cooking is straining the seams of my jeans as it is. It's getting indecent."

"Haven't heard any of the men complaining about the fit of your jeans," Luke drawled.

"Luke!" Carla said, laughing.

"Well, have you heard them complaining?" he asked innocently before switching his attention to Logan. "Hurry up, son. Your old man is ready for dessert."

Carla laughed and murmured something Diana couldn't hear. Silently she retreated from the living room doorway, heading for the kitchen. It wasn't that she felt unwelcome, for she knew that the opposite was the case. Carla and Luke loved to question Diana about the progress of the dig and the pots that Ten and she together had proven to be so adept at assembling from shards. It was just that she wasn't sure she could look at Luke and Carla and their baby without letting her own hunger show.

What a pity it takes a man to make a baby.

It wasn't the first time the thought had occurred to Diana, but the strength of her yearning for a baby was growing. Tonight it had shaken her, making it hard for her to think.

But then, that wasn't new, either. Diana hadn't been thinking too well around Ten lately. A look from him, a phrase, a slight lift of the corner of his mouth, and she would begin thinking all over again about how gentle he had been with the kitten, how patient he was with the fragile, brittle shards, how easy and yet how exciting he was to be with.

Stop it. Next thing you know you'll be asking him to kiss you.

A curious sensation prickled through Diana, making her shiver lightly. She wasn't sure what it was that had caused her reaction. She knew what it wasn't, however.

It wasn't fear.

Diana let herself out into the night. Overhead the Milky Way was a river of light flowing silently across the sky. There was no moon to pale the glitter of the stars, no clouds to blur the razor edges of MacKenzie Ridge's silhouette. Nothing moved but the wind. It infused the night, filling it with whispers that could have been her own thoughts or echoes of ancient Anasazi prayers chanted to unknown gods.

When Diana opened the door to the old ranch house, Pounce materialized from the nearby bushes and slipped into the house ahead of her. She closed the door, bent down and lifted the big tomcat into her arms.

"Hello, Pounce. How was mouse hunting tonight?"

The cat purred and began kneading Diana's chest.

"That good, hmm?" Diana murmured, rubbing the supple body and sleek fur. "Then I won't bother putting out that dry cat food Carla gave me yesterday."

Pounce purred his agreement.

"Yeah, that's what she said. You only eat the dry stuff when nothing else is available."

Sure enough, Pounce ignored the kibble that Diana prepared with one hand while she held on to the cat with the other. Even a saucer of milk didn't interest him. All he wanted was what he was getting—a chance to snuggle with his favorite human being.

Carrying Pounce, Diana walked through the workroom to her bedroom. The carefully made bed looked uninviting. It was too early to sleep. Even if the hour had been right, her frame of mind was not. She was too restless to sleep.

Unfortunately she was also too restless to work on the shards. She tried, but for once the lure of putting together an ancient puzzle couldn't hold her attention. After fitting a few pieces together, she turned off the big gooseneck lamp and sat at the work table with no more illumination than that provided by the lamp in the far corner of the room. The shadows cast by that lamp were soft and inviting, making velvet distinctions between light and dark.

Pounce leaped into Diana's lap and *yeowed* in soft demand. Absently she stroked the cat, drawing forth a ripple of purrs. For a long time there was no other sound. Then a knock came on the front door and Ten called out. Hearing Ten's deep voice sent another curious frisson through Diana.

"I'm in the workroom," she answered.

Her voice was unusually husky, but the words carried well enough. The door opened and closed and Ten walked into the room. With a gesture that had become familiar to her, he removed his hat and set it on the small table beneath the lamp.

"That old mouser must think he's died and gone to heaven," Ten said.

The corner of his mouth tugged up, sending another glimmer of heat through Diana.

"Did you mean what you said?" she asked before she could think of all the reasons to be silent.

"I always mean what I say. When it comes to you and that cat, I'm damned certain."

Diana took a deep breath. "Would you really trade places with Pounce?"

This time the curve at the corner of Ten's mouth expanded into a true smile. "Why? You have some mice that he's too lazy to catch?"

Her lips tried to smile but were trembling too hard. She could barely find the courage to force out her next question.

"Would you really like to be touched by me?" she asked. "I mean, do I . . . attract you?"

"Sure," Ten said offhandedly, reaching for the switch on the gooseneck lamp.

"Would you . . . kiss me?"

Ten's hand froze in midair. Amusement vanished from his expression. His eyes narrowed until there was little left but a silver glitter as he turned and looked at the woman who was only a few feet away.

"You're serious, aren't you," he said.

She nodded because her throat was too tight for words.

"What happened to all the No Trespassing signs?"

Diana opened her mouth. No words came from her constricted throat. She licked her lips. Ten watched the motion with a heavy-lidded, sensual intensity that would have frightened her once. Now it came as a relief. It gave her the courage to put into words the realization that had been growing in her mind for a long time.

"Watching Carla and Luke and their baby has made me understand that I'm missing something wonderful and—and vital." Diana's voice shifted, becoming even lower, more husky. She spoke swiftly, as though afraid of being interrupted and then not having the courage to continue. "But until I get over being afraid of men, I won't have a chance for the kind of life I want. Men want sex. I have to be able to give a man what he wants in order to get what I really want—a baby of my own."

Ten's left eyebrow rose in a wicked black arch. "Honey, you don't need a man to get a baby." His mouth tugged up at the corner in response to Diana's shocked look. "If you don't believe me, ask any veterinarian."

Silky hair flew as Diana shook her head vigorously. "No. That's not what I want. Too cold. I want my baby to be conceived in warmth, in a—a joining of two people. Not a doctor's office. That wouldn't—I just—no." She took a fast, harsh breath, trying to control her nervousness. "So I have to start somewhere. A kiss seems a logical beginning."

"Why me?"

Diana looked away, unable to bear the diamond clarity of Ten's eyes.

"Because I—I trust you," she said, her voice uneven. "I've seen you handle kittens and delicate pieces of pottery. You're as gentle as you are strong. When I was trapped in the kiva, I was helpless, completely at your mercy. You could have done anything, but what you did was pull me out, comfort me, take care of me. Never once did you so much as hint that I owed you thanks, much less the use of my body for sex.''

Unwavering gray eyes watched Diana. ''And now you want me to kiss you?''

Closing her eyes, she nodded.

''Despite your fear of men,'' Ten added.

Again, she nodded. Then, in a whispered rush, she said, ''I like you, Ten. I know I could bear being kissed by you, but the thought of any other man makes me—cold.''

A visible shudder of fear and revulsion went through Diana. Ten saw it but said nothing.

''Anyway,'' she added with desperate calm, ''if you know going in that all it's going to be is a kiss, you won't push for more, will you? If I'm honest?'' Diana opened her eyes and looked at Ten with unconscious pleading. ''I'm not a tease. Truly. It's just that I can't bear being touched by men.''

''What happened?'' Ten asked calmly. ''Why do you have such a poor opinion of sex in general and men in particular? What makes you afraid that every man you kiss will demand sex?''

''Because it's true.''

''You don't believe that.''

''The hell I don't,'' she said, her voice low and flat.

Ten stared at Diana. All her softness and unconscious pleading was gone, all hope, all color; and what was left was a bleak acceptance that made her voice as flat as the line of her mouth.

''Look,'' Ten said reasonably, ''no man worthy of the name is going to share a few kisses with a woman and then demand a turn in the sack.''

Diana shrugged. The movement was tight, jerky, saying more than words about the tension within her, a tension that had been pulling her apart for too many years.

"Maybe you're right," she said. Then she made an angry, anguished sound. Years of bitterness burst out in a torrent of words. "But the only way to find out which men are decent is to try the kisses, all the while praying very hard that when the time comes he'll take no for an answer, because if he doesn't, he's bigger than you are, stronger, and you've been dating him for months and no one on earth will believe that he forced you."

"You're acting as though all men—"

"Not *all* men," she interrupted savagely. "But too damned many! If you don't believe me, ask the psychologist who did a study for UCLA. The statistics are illuminating. More than a third of all women have their first sexual experience as the result of rape."

"What?"

"Rape," Diana said savagely. "I'm not talking about being beaten senseless or having a knife at your throat until the rapist is finished, although God knows I talked to too many girls who got initiated that way, in outright violence."

Diana's breath came in harshly, but she gave Ten no chance to speak. "I'm not even talking about incest. I'm talking about the dumb middle-class bunnies who believe that no means no, who believe that the boy they've been dating for three months won't use his strength against his girlfriend, won't keep pushing and pushing and pushing her for sex, taking off her clothes while she says no, putting his hand between her legs even when she tries to push it away, and each time they're alone he pushes harder and harder until finally he was holding me down, telling me all the while how it was okay, nice girls did it all the time, he'd still love me in the morning, in fact he'd love me more than ever—"

"Diana," Ten said, his voice low, shocked.

She didn't even hear him. "—and I was too well brought up to claw and scream and kick, and above all *I couldn't believe Steve wouldn't stop.* Nice middle-class girls don't get raped by nice middle-class boys. He had stopped the times before. He would stop this time. He had to. He simply had to. God help me, I still didn't believe it when he was finished and I was bleeding and he was zipping up his pants suggesting we have a burger and some fries before we went to his apartment and did it some more.''

Diana blinked, shuddered again and made a broken sound. ''To this day Steve doesn't know why I broke our engagement. The last time I talked to him, he got mad and said if I didn't want sex, I shouldn't ask for it by wearing heels and sexy hairstyles and perfume and I shouldn't make out at all. I was a good middle-class girl, so I believed him. I believed it had been my fault.''

Diana's hands clenched until her nails dug into her palms, but her voice remained the same, flat and without warmth. ''When I could bring myself to date again—it took more than a year—I was very careful not to lead a man on. No makeup. No perfume. No skirts. A few kisses, that was all, and then only after several dates. It didn't matter. Two of my dates called me a tease. Some called me worse.''

Pounce made a soft sound of complaint and leaped to the floor, sensing the tension in Diana. She didn't notice the cat's absence.

Neither did Ten. He was still caught in the moment of shock and rage when he had realized why Diana feared men. He heard her words only at a distance. His hands clenched and unclenched reflexively as he tried to reason with himself, to drain off the useless rage that was consuming him. What had happened to Diana had taken place a long time ago. Years.

But for Ten, it had happened just a few seconds ago.

''Only one of the men came back for more than a few dates,'' Diana continued tonelessly, determined to tell Ten everything so that no more questions would have to be asked or answered. ''Don never pushed me. Not once. Not in any way. Eight months later he asked me to marry him, and he told me about how perfect it would be, two virgins learning together the ultimate mystery of sex on their marriage night." She made a helpless gesture with her right hand. "He was a kind, decent man. I couldn't lie to him. So I told him."

When Ten spoke, his voice was as carefully controlled as the coiled strength of his body. "What happened?"

"He tried to believe it wasn't my fault, but when he found out I hadn't gone to the police..." The downward curve of Diana's mouth became more pronounced. "We saw each other a few more times after that, but it was over."

"Did you love him?"

Slowly Diana shook her head. "I didn't love Steve, either. I just wanted to believe it was possible for a man and a woman to share something beautiful, that a man can be decent and civilized with a woman who is weaker than himself."

"I take it your father wasn't."

"My father was a soldier. A commando."

Ten's eyes widened but he said nothing.

"Dad was short-tempered when he was sober. When he drank, he was violent. The older I got, the more he drank. He and Mom..." Diana's voice died. "I never understood why she stayed with him. But she did."

"He's dead?"

"Yes." Diana looked up at Ten for the first time since she had begun talking about her past. "Steve was a jet jockey for the air force. I haven't had very good luck with soldiers. Any more questions?"

"Just one."

Diana braced herself. "Go on."

"Do you still want me to kiss you?"

Nervously Diana smoothed the soft folds of her oversize cotton sweater. She tried to speak, decided she didn't trust her voice, and nodded her head.

"You're sure?" Ten asked.

There was no emotion in his voice, no expression on his face, nothing to tell Diana what he was thinking. He was as dark and enigmatic as the windswept night, and like the stars, his eyes were a glittering silver.

"Yes," she whispered. "I'm sure."

Ten held out his hand. "Then come to me, Diana."

Eleven

Diana trembled at the sound of Ten's voice, a gentle velvet rasp, like a cat's tongue stroking her. For an instant she didn't know if she would have the strength to walk. But even as the thought came she was standing up, walking, closing the small distance that separated her from Ten. She put her hand in his. The warmth of his hard palm was like a flame against fingers chilled by nervousness.

Ten held out his other hand. A moment later, small cool fingers nestled against the cupped heat of his palm. He lifted Diana's hands to his mouth and breathed warmth over her skin before kissing her palms gently. The unexpected caress made Diana's breath break. Before the sweet sensations had run their course through her body, Ten was lowering her hands, releasing her from his warmth.

Diana had asked to be kissed. He had kissed her. She made a questioning sound that had more disappointment in it than she realized.

"Ten?"

"What?" he asked softly.

"Would you kiss me again?" she whispered.

Ten's smile made Diana want to curl up in his arms like a
cat.

He held out his hands and once more felt her smooth,
cool fingers come to rest within the curve of his palms.

"You're so warm," Diana said. She closed her eyes and
let out her breath in a long sigh, openly savoring the simple
touch of her skin against Ten's.

Diana's unguarded, sensual response sent a shock wave of
heat through Ten. He hoped she had no idea how fiercely
she aroused him with her unknowing sensuality and haunted
eyes, her womanly curves badly concealed beneath a sweater
big enough for him to wear, and her slender hands lying so
trustingly within his.

Ten brought Diana's hands to his mouth and brushed a
kiss into first one of her palms, then the other. The tiny
sound she made at the touch of his lips was as much a reward as the warmth he could feel stealing softly beneath her
skin. He lifted his head and looked at her. She was watching him with eyes that were luminous, approving. Then her
dark lashes lowered and she returned the kisses he had given
her, breathing a caress into the center of his palm.

"Thank you," Diana whispered.

"My pleasure."

She searched Ten's face with wide indigo eyes, hardly able
to believe what her senses were telling her. He had enjoyed
the undemanding caresses as much as she had.

"You mean that, don't you," she said finally.

Ten nodded.

"It's a relief to find a man who doesn't want...
everything."

An odd smile haunted Ten's lips for a moment. "Don't
fool yourself, Diana. I want everything, but I'll never *take*
any more than you give me. And I mean give willingly, not
because I push you so hard on so many fronts at once that
you don't know where to fight first."

Diana smiled uncertainly. "Does that mean you'll kiss me again?"

"I'll kiss you as many times as you want me to."

"And you won't push for more?"

"No."

"Even if you get aroused?" The stark question shocked Diana when she heard her own words, but it was too late to call them back.

"Honey," Ten said, his voice rich with rueful laughter, "if you were standing about two inches closer to me, you'd have the answer to your question."

Confusion showed on Diana's face. Without thinking, she looked down Ten's body. The evidence of his arousal was unmistakable and frankly intimidating. She looked up again, her face suddenly pale.

"Don't worry, honey," Ten said matter-of-factly. "I've been that way every night we've sat around talking and sorting through pieces of the past, and more often than not during the days, too."

"You have?" she asked faintly. "I didn't know."

"I did my best to make sure of that," Ten said dryly. "I'm only pointing it out now so that you'll know you don't have to be afraid of me when I'm aroused."

"But I didn't mean to. Believe me, Ten. I didn't mean anything of the sort!"

"I know. I can't keep myself from responding to you, but I can make damn sure I don't act on it."

"But if I didn't mean to, why..." Her voice faded. "Has it been so long since you've had a woman?"

Ten looked at Diana's confusion and didn't know whether to laugh or swear. Very lightly he stroked his index finger over the inside of her wrist. The touch was gentle but hardly soothing. He felt her pulse rate accelerate, which made his own quicken in response.

"Diana, I could have had a woman five seconds before I walk into a room where you are and I'd still want you. I admire courage, intelligence and a sense of humor. It didn't take long for me to find out that you've got plenty of all three, as well as a fine body you do your best to hide.''

Color crept up Diana's cheeks, but she made no move to separate her hands from Ten's while he continued talking in the velvet tones that made her weak.

''I've wanted you since the first day you were here, when you put your own uneasiness aside and helped me with that kitten.''

Diana's eyes widened in surprise.

''I respect a woman's right to choose or refuse a man,'' Ten continued. ''You made it clear that you were refusing. You're still making it clear. You're as safe as you want to be with me, no matter what kind of kissing or petting we do.''

She barely heard what Ten was saying. She was still trying to absorb the realization that he was more aroused than Steve had ever been, yet Ten had made no move toward easing himself at her expense. Nor had he berated her for teasing him into such an uncomfortable state and then refusing to follow through.

Then the rest of what Ten was saying sank in: *You're as safe as you want to be with me, no matter what kind of kissing or petting we do.*

She didn't doubt it. Despite the provocation Baker had given—and the pothunters—Ten had never lost control over his own actions.

''Where did you learn such self-control?'' Diana asked, watching Ten with dark, curious eyes.

''The same place I learned how to fight.''

''That kind of training didn't do my father any good. Or Steve.''

Ten banked the rage that came to him whenever he thought of a man hurting Diana. ''They weren't men, honey. They were boys who never learned the most important part of a warrior's training—self-control. If a man doesn't control himself, someone else will. There are times and places where being out of control can cost a man his life. Your father was lucky. He was never in one of those places. As for Steve, if that fly-boy's luck holds, I'll never meet him.''

Ten's voice was so caressing that for an instant the meaning of what he was saying didn't make any impact. When it did, Diana looked quickly at Ten's eyes. There was nothing of amusement or indulgence there, only the icy promise of retribution she had seen twice before in Ten's eyes—and each time a man had ended up flat on the ground with Ten towering over him.

"Now I've frightened you," Ten said, stepping back, releasing Diana. "I'd never hurt you, but after your experiences with the male of the species, I don't expect you to believe that." He turned toward the gooseneck lamp, reaching for the switch. "Let's take a look at those new red shards you got out of the carton." Ten hesitated, glancing at Diana over his shoulder. "Or would you feel more at ease if I left you to work alone?"

Diana's hand went to Ten's, covering his fingers, preventing him from turning on the harsh light. She tugged lightly. He let go of the switch, allowing her to control his hand. She lifted it to her face. Closing her eyes, she stroked his hard palm with her cheek.

"Diana?"

"It's all right."

"Is it? Your hands are trembling."

Helplessly she smiled. "I don't know why they are, but I know it's not fear."

"Are you sure, honey?"

"I know what being afraid of a man feels like. I'm not afraid of you, Ten."

He searched Diana's eyes for a long moment, then gave her a slow smile that did nothing to steady her heartbeat or her hands. Watching him, trying to smile in return even though her lips were trembling, she found Ten's other hand and brought it to her mouth for a quick brush of her lips. Then she turned her other cheek into his palm, framing her face in his warmth, holding his hands against her skin.

"Ten," Diana said huskily, closing her eyes, savoring the slow caress of his fingers, "will you share a few kisses with me until I ask you to stop? I know this isn't fair to you, but—"

"It's all right," he said, interrupting, his lips against Diana's, feeling them tremble against his own. "Life is never fair. You of all people should know that."

"But—"

"Shh," Ten said, sealing her lips with a tender stroking of his thumb. "It's all right, baby."

Diana's eyes opened. Indigo depths shimmered with the possibilities that were unfolding within her, possibilities that existed because of the powerful man who was holding her with such care.

"Kiss me," she whispered.

"How?" he asked in a velvet voice. "Hard or gentle? Deep or cool? Fast or so long that you can't remember a time when we weren't kissing? I've never had that kind of kiss, but looking at you, I believe it exists."

Diana's eyes widened and she shivered lightly at the thought of trying each and every way of kissing Ten.

"How do you want to kiss me?" she asked.

"Every way there is."

"Yes," she sighed.

Ten's breath came out in a husky rush that Diana felt an instant before his lips touched hers. His lips were smooth and incredibly soft, fitting over hers tenderly yet completely. He brushed against her mouth again and again, letting her become accustomed to his textures, enjoying hers in return, and what he enjoyed most of all was the way her lips began to follow his, silently asking for more.

Smiling, ignoring the heavy beat of his own blood, Ten gave Diana more of the undemanding caresses. Her mouth relaxed and softened and her breath sighed between her slightly parted lips. The tip of his tongue touched the sensitive peak of her upper lip, then withdrew, only to return and touch her again. She made a murmurous sound and tilted her face more fully up to his. Her reward was a warm, gliding caress that went from corner to corner of her smile. She made another low sound that became a tiny cry of surprise when his teeth closed tenderly on her lower lip, holding it captive. Instantly he released her and began the elusive, gliding kisses all over again.

"Ten," Diana said, the word more a sigh than his name.

"Too much?"

"No." Her teeth closed a little less than gently on Ten's lower lip. She heard his breath break and released him, whispering, "Not enough."

"Does that mean you won't run if I taste that beautiful mouth?"

"Yes."

"The way you were hanging on to my hands, I wasn't sure."

Belatedly, Diana realized that she was imprisoning Ten's hands against her face, holding him hard enough to leave marks on his tanned skin.

"I'm sorry," she said quickly, releasing his hands. "When you started kissing me I forgot everything else."

Ten bent and touched a corner of her mouth with his tongue. "That's all right, honey. I just thought you might be worried that I'd start straying out of bounds if you let go of my hands."

"What?"

"Don't you remember high school? Nothing below the collarbone in front or the waist in back."

Diana started to laugh, but the look in Ten's eyes took her breath away. His words were light, his voice was velvet, but his eyes were a smoldering gray that made her knees weak.

"I remember."

"That's the way it will be for us. If you want my hands anywhere else, you'll have to put them there."

"But then you would—you would expect more."

"I expect to spend this night like I've spent every night since I pulled you out of that kiva—hungry as hell. That's my problem, not yours. You've done nothing to encourage me.''

"Nothing? What about right now?''

"This isn't encouraging.'' Ten lowered his mouth another fraction of an inch. His teeth closed tenderly on Diana's lower lip. The tip of his tongue caressed her captive flesh until she made a small sound at the back of her throat. He released her, gave her a quick, biting kiss and looked at her flushed lips with hunger. "This is pleasure, honey, pure and simple.''

"Steve always—he said it hurt him.''

Ten's answer was another brush of his lips against Diana's, but this time there was no lifting, no gliding, no teasing. His fingers eased into her hair, rubbing her scalp, holding her with gentle care while he joined their mouths in a different kind of kiss. The caressing pressure of his lips increased, tilting her head back, yet still she felt no uneasiness.

Slender fingers threaded into the thick pelt of Ten's hair, holding him even closer, wanting the kiss not to end. When Diana murmured his name, he accepted the invitation of her parted lips. His tongue glided between her teeth, seeking the moist heat beyond, finding it in a slow, deep tasting that was like nothing she had ever known. He memorized the contours of her mouth with teasing, sliding touches, caressing her, enjoying her, cherishing her. Only when she whimpered and pressed even closer to his body did he complete the seduction of her mouth.

Diana had never realized just how sensitive her tongue was, how it could discriminate so vividly between the satin smoothness and intriguing serrations of Ten's teeth, the silken texture and beguiling heat of his mouth, the nubby velvet enticement of his tongue sliding against hers in a dance of penetration and retreat that made her forget who was stronger, who was weaker, who was frightened and who was not. Tender and sweet, hot and wild, the kiss shimmered with both restraint and the sensuous consummation of two mouths completely joined.

Diana was never certain who ended the kiss or if it had truly ended at all. Slowly she realized that her arms were around Ten's neck, his arms were around her, supporting her and arching her into his body at the same time, and he was looking at her mouth as though he had just discovered fire.

"Ten?"

The huskiness of Diana's voice made his whole body tighten. Her heavy-lidded, luminous eyes told him that she had been as deeply involved in the kiss as he had. When she looked at his mouth and her own lips parted in unconscious invitation, Ten made a sound that was part laugh, part groan and all male.

"Do you want to taste me again?" he asked.

The shiver of response that went through Diana was clearly felt by Ten.

"Then take me," he said huskily.

Indigo eyes widened for a startled moment, then her lashes swept down as she looked at Ten's mouth. Her breath rushed out in a sigh that he tasted in the instant before she took his mouth, relearning his textures in a sharing of tongues that had neither beginning nor end, simply the hushed intimacy of their quickened breaths intermingling with the night.

Diana's last thought before the kiss ended was wonder that she could tremble and yet know not the least bit of fear. She had never felt so safe in her life . . . or so sweetly threatened.

Twelve

"Not a chance," Ten said flatly. "If you think I'm letting you excavate that kiva, you're crazy." He pulled Diana out of the truck and shut the door hard behind her. "You're not going anywhere near that hole."

Diana blinked and stared at the man who had suddenly become every inch the ramrod of the Rocking M rather than the restrained lover who last night had taught her the pleasure of being kissed. Just kissed. All through the long drive to September Canyon, memories had come at odd times, making her shiver; then she would look over at Ten and he would smile at her, knowing what she was thinking.

He wasn't smiling now. Neither his stance nor the taut power of his body suggested that there was a bit of gentleness in him.

"I want your promise on that, Diana."

She waited for the fear that had always come to her in the past when a man had stood hard-shouldered in front of her, his very size a threat that didn't have to be spoken aloud.

"Or else?" she asked tightly.

"Or else we've had a long drive out here for nothing, because we're going back."

"And if I refuse to go back?"

"You'll go anyway."

Diana looked at Ten's gray eyes and wondered how she had ever thought of them as warm, much less hot enough to set fires.

"Ramrod. It does suit you."

He waited.

"I'll stay on this side of the canyon," Diana said angrily. "You have my word on it. Not that you need it. You could enforce your edict and you damn well know it."

"Could I?" Ten asked in a cool voice. "You're smart and quick. You could find a way to go exploring before I could stop you. But now that you've given your word, I won't wake up in a cold sweat, seeing you lying beneath stone, only this time you aren't moving, this time you don't get up and walk away."

Diana felt the blood leave her face. She made a small sound and reached for him.

"Ten?" she whispered, touching his face.

He closed his eyes for an instant. When they opened again, they were alive once more. He bent and kissed Diana's upturned mouth quickly, then more slowly. When he lifted his mouth he whispered, "I'm glad you weren't afraid of me just now."

"I wasn't?"

Ten framed Diana's face between his large hands. "You dug in and gave as good as you got. Then you decided that it wasn't worth a long drive back to the ranch, so you agreed. That's not fear, honey. That's common sense. Me, now. I was scared."

Diana laughed in his face.

"It's true," he said. "I was afraid you'd be frightened of me and then you wouldn't let me kiss you again."

Memories of the previous night rose up in Diana, sending heat glittering from her breasts to her knees.

"What sweet sounds you make," Ten murmured, listening to the soft breaking of her breath. "Will you panic if I put my arms around you and give you the kind of kiss I wanted to give you this morning?"

Her breath came out in a long rush. "I've been hoping you would. I know it sounds crazy, but I feel like it's been forever since I kissed you. I miss your taste, Ten. I miss it until I ache."

"Open your mouth for me, honey," he whispered. "I missed you the same way, aching with it."

The heat and sweetness of Ten's mouth locked with Diana's. His taste swept through her, stealing her breath, her thoughts. Her arms tightened around his neck as she sought to get closer to him, then closer still. Soft sounds came from her throat as she gave in to a sweeping need to hold him so fiercely that he couldn't let go of her until his kiss had soothed the aching that had made sleep elude her through the long hours of the night.

Gravity slipped, then vanished, leaving Diana suspended within the hard warmth of Ten's arms. With catlike pleasure she kneaded the flexed muscles of his arms and shoulders, urging him to hold her more tightly, not caring if she could breathe. She felt no fear at the blunt reality of Ten's strength closing around her in a hot, sensual vise, for that was what she wanted, what she had ached for without knowing why or how.

Not until Diana was dizzy from lack of air did she permit the kiss to end, and even then she clung to Ten, her face against the sultry skin of his neck, her body shaking with each breath.

"Oh, baby," Ten said, shuddering with the force of his violent self-restraint. "There's a fire in you that could make stone burn. If you ever want more than kissing from a man, come to me."

Diana made an inarticulate sound and pressed her mouth against the corded tension of Ten's neck. The touch of her tongue on his skin went through him like lightning.

"You taste good," she said slowly, touching him again with her tongue. "Salty. Does your skin taste like that everywhere, or just on your neck?"

Desire ripped through Ten as he thought of his whole body being tasted by Diana's innocent, incendiary tongue. Very carefully he lowered her until she could stand on her own feet. He forced himself not to look at her reddened lips and cheeks flushed by desire. He wanted her until he was shaking with it. He had never wanted a woman like that. And that, too, shook him.

"Ten?"

"If you want to get any sketching done, we'd better unload the truck. You'll lose the best light."

"Sweet light."

Ten lifted a single dark eyebrow.

"That's what photographers call late-afternoon light," Diana explained. "Sweet light."

An image came to Ten of Diana wearing only slanting gold light, the womanly curves of her body glowing and her husky voice asking him to touch her. With an effort he banished the image, forcing himself to concentrate on what must be done.

"Where do you want to sketch first?" he asked. His voice was too thick, but he could do nothing about that for a few minutes, any more than he could quickly banish the hard proof of his hunger for her.

"I've done all the close-ups of the ruins I can do until the grads clear out more rubble and excavate to a new level," Diana said. "I need to do some perspective sketches, showing the ruins in relation to their natural environment, but to do that, I've got to be on the opposite side of the canyon."

Shrugging, Diana said nothing more. She had agreed not to cross over to the other side of the canyon, which meant that she had no sketches to do at the moment.

Silently Ten swore, knowing his reluctance to let her near
the kiva was irrational.

"Get your sketching gear together. I'll go over the area
myself. If nothing else gives way, you can sketch anywhere
you like. Just make sure I'm within calling distance. And
don't go near that damned kiva."

Fifteen minutes later Ten and Diana had unloaded the
truck and were ready to go. He set out for the ruins at a pace
that made her work hard to keep up. She didn't complain.
One look at the line of Ten's jaw told her that he wasn't
pleased to be leading her back toward the kiva.

Within a few minutes Diana was tasting the same kind of
dread that had haunted Ten. Watching him quarter the area
at the bottom of the cliff where she had fallen through,
waiting for him to stumble into an ancient trap, standing
with breath held until she ached; it was all Diana could do
not to call Ten back even though she knew that the chance
of his finding another intact kiva was so small as to be in-
significant.

The chance had been equally small for her, and she had
stepped through the roof of a kiva anyway.

Half an hour passed before Ten was satisfied that the
terrain concealed no more traps. If there were any other kivas, they had been filled in by dirt long ago or their ceilings
were still strong enough to carry his one hundred and eighty
pounds. Either way, Diana should be safe. The kiva she had
fallen into on her first day was a hundred feet distant, clearly
marked by stakes.

Ten signaled for Diana to join him. She scrambled up the
rugged slope with the offhanded grace of a deer. Very
quickly she was standing close enough for Ten to sense the
heat of her body.

"Find anything?" she asked breathlessly.

"Potshards, masonry rubble and that."

Diana followed the direction of Ten's thumb. It took her
a moment to realize what she was seeing. Sometime in the
past five to eight hundred years, a piece of the cliff had

fallen, all but filling the alcove below. Once the opening had held rooms. Now it held only an immense mound of cracked, broken sandstone. Water seeped in tiny rivulets from beneath the stone, telling of a spring hidden beneath. Her trained eye quickly picked out the angular stones and random potshards that marked an Anasazi site.

"I hope they were already gone when the cliff came down," Diana said in a low voice, remembering what Ten had said.

. . . lying beneath stone, only this time you aren't moving, this time you don't get up and walk away.

Ten's big hand stroked her head from crown to neck. "Somehow," he said slowly, "I don't think they were. In fact, I'm...certain." He caressed her sensitive nape with the ball of his thumb before he lifted his hand and stepped away. "Better get sketching, honey. Even stone doesn't last forever."

Intent and relaxed at the same time, Diana sketched quickly, not wanting to lose the effect of slanting afternoon light on the ruins across the canyon. At her urging, Ten had crossed the small creek again and stood looking toward the ruins, giving scale to the cliff and the ragged lines of once whole rooms.

"Just a few more minutes," she called.

Ten waved his understanding. Diana's pencil flew over the paper as she added texture and definition to cliffs and canyon bottom, cottonwood and brush. The heightened contrast gave an almost eerie depth to the sketch.

The drawings she had made before had been accurate representations of the ruins as they were today. The drawing she was working on now was a re-creation of the ruins as they had looked long ago, when the sound of barking dogs, domesticated turkeys and children's laughter had echoed through the canyon, a time when women ground corn in stone metates or painted intricate designs on pottery while their men discussed the weather or the gods or the latest rumor of raids from the north. The narrow canyon would have been alive with voices then, especially on a day like today, when the sun was hot and vital, pouring light and life over the land.

Yet today, despite Diana's usual custom, she wasn't sketching people among the buildings. Nor was she sketching the burning blue radiance of the sky. There were heavy clouds surrounding the sole figure in her drawing, a man standing on the margin of the creek. The man was both dark and compelling, black hair lifting on a storm wind, an outlaw shaman calling to his brother the storm.

The power of the man was revealed in the taut male lines of shoulder and waist, buttocks and legs, a strength that was rooted in the center of the earth and in a past when the lives of humans and spirits had been intertwined. Standing with his back to the collapsed alcove, the shaman was a still center in the swirling violence of the wind. His brother the storm had answered the shaman's call.

The shaman turned around and looked at Diana with eyes the color of rain, eyes that saw past the surface of reality to the soul beneath.

Diana shivered, blinked, and realized that she had been staring at the finished drawing so intently that her body was cramped in protest. Automatically she flipped the sketch tablet closed, both protecting and concealing the drawing. She slipped the tablet into its carrying case and stood up. Moments later she was hurrying down the slope toward Ten.

He turned at the sound of her approach, watching her with eyes the color of rain.

"Finished already?" Ten asked, holding out his hand to take Diana's pack.

She gave him her hand instead. Slowly he laced their fingers together until their hands were palm to palm. The sensitive inner skin of her fingers felt the hard pressure of him everywhere. The slow, complete interlocking was as intimate as a kiss. His palm was warm and hardened by work, making her wonder how it would feel on her skin if he were given the freedom of her body.

The thought haunted Diana while she and Ten went through their normal end-of-the-day chores—a basin bath behind the screen, then preparing dinner and cleaning up the campsite. Although the sun had vanished behind stone cliffs, true sunset was still an hour away. Shadows flowing out from the rocks had taken the edge off the unusual heat of the day, but the canyon walls still radiated the captured warmth of the sun.

Diana felt no need to pull her customary loose sweater over the sleeveless cotton blouse she was wearing. In fact, after her camp bath she had substituted sandals and shorts for hiking boots and jeans. Ten was feeling the heat, too. After his bath he hadn't bothered to put on a shirt or socks and boots. At the moment he was stretched out on his bedroll, which he had moved to the edge of the overhang, hoping to catch a vagrant breeze.

"Too bad we're not camping at Black Springs," Ten said, stretching slowly, fully. "There are pools big enough to cool off in."

"Sounds like heaven. Not that I'm complaining," Diana added, frowning over a handful of shards. "I've been at sites where the only water we had was strictly for drinking."

She turned away from the shards she had been sorting, saw Ten sprawled with feline ease across his bedroll and felt an increasingly familiar glittering sensation from her breasts to her knees. Without stopping to think, she walked over and sat next to him.

"Ten?"

His eyes opened. They were a burning silver.

Diana's thoughts scattered, and with them her ability to speak coherently. "Can I—that is, would you—could we—?"

"I thought you'd never ask."

Large hands closed around Diana's face, bringing her closer. Their mouths fitted together smoothly, seamlessly, and at the first taste of each other they both made low sounds of pleasure. Ten's hands shifted, lifting Diana, easing her across his chest until most of her weight was pressed against him. The shiver that went through her was as clear as lightning at midnight. He groaned and released her.

"Dammit, honey," Ten said heavily. "I didn't mean to frighten you. I didn't think how you would feel being on a man's bed again, and me half-naked at that."

Diana shook her head. "It wasn't in a bed. It was the front seat of a car. That's why I always sit so far away in the truck. And he never—never completely took off his clothes. Or mine."

Ten closed his eyes so that she wouldn't see the rage tugging against his control. He held her gently against his chest, stroking her head and back, kissing her hair, wishing that he could change the past.

But he could not. He could only hold Diana and want her until it was a kind of agony.

The slow stroking of Ten's hand sent currents of pleasure through Diana, making her breath sigh out. She smoothed her cheek against his chest, encountered a resilient cushion of hair instead of cloth, and made a murmurous sound of discovery. Ten's hand hesitated, then continued its languid journey from the silky hair of her head to the intriguing line of her back. Though the pressure was unchanged, the caress was different, sensual rather than soothing, enticing rather than calming. He felt the heat of her breath on his breastbone as she kissed him lingeringly. Then he felt her lips open. She hesitated.

"Go ahead," Ten said. "Find out if I taste the same there as I did on my neck."

Diana lifted her head until she could see his eyes. "You won't mind?"

His smile was slow, hot, infinitely male. "Baby, you can put that sweet mouth anywhere on me that you want."

Deep blue eyes widened in shock and . . . curiosity. The shock he had expected. The curiosity made him want to pull her hard against his body and show her just how much he wouldn't mind any damn thing she wanted to do to him.

The first, exploring touch of Diana's tongue made Ten's breath stick in his throat. He had expected a darting taste followed by a smart comment about the limitations of camp baths. He hadn't expected a sleek, hot foray through the thicket of his chest hair. He hadn't expected her purring sounds of pleasure as she tasted him. Most of all, he hadn't expected her nipples to harden against him when she found and caressed his own nipple to a tiny, aching point.

Ten lay rigidly, fighting his own arousal and the sudden, violent need to touch Diana, to hold the sweet weight of her breasts in his hands, to taste and suckle and tease her until she writhed in an agony of pleasure. But all he permitted himself to do was slide the fingers of his left hand deeply into Diana's hair, holding her mouth against him while his right hand kneaded her back from nape to waist, pressing her even closer to the growing heat of his body. When he could bear no more he eased her mouth back up his chest until he could slide his tongue between her teeth, kissing her deeply, drinking her, mating with her in the only way she would allow.

By the time Ten released Diana's mouth she could barely think, much less speak. Her lips felt flushed, full, sated, but the rest of her body ached.

"I want—more than kissing," she said. "But I don't know how much more."

"It's all right," Ten said, kissing Diana's lips gently. "We'll take it slow and easy. The only rule will be the oldest and best one of all. Anytime I do something you don't want, tell me. I'll stop."

"That isn't fair to you. Yes, I know," she said quickly, before Ten could speak. "Life isn't fair. But I don't want to make it any harder on you."

The left corner of Ten's mouth tugged up. "Honey, it can't get any harder than it already is." He brushed another kiss over Diana's mouth, scattering her objections.

Moving slowly, he lifted her from his body and stretched her out on her side with her back to him. "You'll feel safer this way, nothing in front of you, nothing holding you down, nothing trapping you. Just me behind you, and you know I'd never take you by surprise, don't you?"

"Y-yes," Diana said. It was the truth. If she hadn't trusted Ten at an instinctive level, she wouldn't even be in September Canyon with him, much less still shivering from his kisses. She let out a long breath that she hadn't been aware of holding and realized that Ten had been right about another thing. She did feel safer lying on her side with nothing in front of her but the view of a canyon slowly succumbing to the embrace of twilight. The setting couldn't have been farther from her memories of being wedged between cold machinery and Steve's relentless body. "Ten?"

"Hmm?"

"You're right. I feel safer this way."

"Good," Ten murmured, glad that Diana's back was to him, for it gave him the freedom to look at the line of her waist flaring into her rounded hips and then tapering slowly to her ankles. If she had seen the hunger and male approval in his eyes as he looked at her, she might have felt less relaxed with her back to him.

Ten's long index finger traced the line of Diana's body from the crown of her head, over her right ear, down her neck, over her right shoulder, down her ribs to her waist, up the rise of her hips, then down every bit of her right leg to her ankle. The primal ripple of her response followed his caress, telling Ten that her whole body had become sensitized to passion.

"That," he said, kissing the nape of Diana's neck, "broke every one of the high school rules about collarbones and waist. Feel like bolting yet?"

Thirteen

***

Diana laughed shakily, wondering at the curious weakness that had followed Ten's caress. He had broken the rules, but in such a way as not to touch any of the forbidden areas.

"Does that little laugh mean I can do it again?" Ten asked.

The subdued humor in Ten's voice was another kind of reassurance to Diana. Steve had been deadly serious whenever they had been alone, intent on getting as much from her sexually as he could, as quickly as he could.

"Yes," Diana whispered.

A shiver of response followed the seductive movement of Ten's fingertip from Diana's head to her heels. This time he slid beneath her arm, as well, caressing the sensitive skin.

"You're a pleasure to touch," Ten said, kissing Diana's nape again. "Soft, resilient, alive." His tongue traced the line of her scalp to her ear. He smiled to hear the sudden intake of her breath. "You have the sweetest curves. Here," he said, biting her ear gently. "And here." His fingers curled around her arm caressingly. When his fingers moved on, his mouth lingered. He kissed the bare skin of her arm, biting softly, drawing tiny sounds from her. "And here."

Ten's hand shaped the tightly drawn line of her waist, kneading lightly, then more firmly. Slowly, inevitably, his palm moved over the full curve of Diana's hip. "And here." His fingers fanned out, shaping her. As his teeth closed over her nape, his hand flexed into her resilient flesh, luxuriating in the feel of her.

The unexpected caress drew a ragged sound from Diana. Currents of sensation rippled through her, making her want to shift restlessly. She stirred, and her movements acted to increase the pressure of Ten's hand. When his palm smoothed down her bare thigh, she forgot to be worried that he would slide his fingers between her legs. Only when his hand had stroked over her calves to her ankles did she realize that the danger zone had been bypassed once more.

Ten continued the slow, undemanding sweeps of his hand up and down Diana's body. The long caresses were punctuated by his teeth biting gently at her nape, her shoulder, the elegant line of her back; and each time his hand traveled back up her body, he skimmed closer to the shadowed secrets between her thighs and the fullness of her breasts. He explored the smooth curve of her belly with slow pressures that eased her hips back into the muscular cradle of his legs. The pressure of her against his fiercely aroused flesh was a sweet fire that made his hands shake.

Breath held against a groan, Ten waited for Diana to retreat. When she didn't, he pressed her even closer, savoring the pleasure-pain of his own need for a moment before he released her, not wanting to frighten her. His hand shifted, stroking slowly up the center line of her body, giving her every chance to refuse the growing intimacy of his touch.

Buttons caught and tugged against Ten's hand. He made no move to undo them despite his aching desire to touch Diana without the barrier of cloth. He simply caressed her from navel to breastbone to neck and back again, follow-

ing the center of her body, knowing only a hint of the
womanly curves that were calling to him.

"Wait," she said huskily.

Immediately Ten's hand stopped, then withdrew. Before
he could retreat farther, slender fingers covered his, holding his hand against her belly. Her shoulders moved, her
fingers urged his—and suddenly Ten found his hand inside
Diana's blouse, cupping the lush weight of her breast. A
groan was pulled from his throat, a low sound of desire that
mingled with the one she made as her nipple peaked in a
rush of sensation that left her weak.

Diana's breath unraveled into broken sighs as Ten's hand
moved slowly from one breast to the other, caressing her,
cherishing her. When his finger slid beneath the thin fabric
of her bra and circled the tip of one breast, she gasped at the
unexpected pleasure. He teased her nipple again, then
withdrew, leaving her aching for more.

"Ten?"

He made a sound that could have been "More?"

"Yes," she sighed.

A long finger skimmed over Diana's nipple again, but the
sensation was much less acute, because there was cloth between them this time. Without stopping to think, she released the front fastening of her bra, baring herself to Ten's
touch.

A hammer blow of desire went through Ten, making his
hands shake. He eased one long arm beneath Diana's head,
cradling her and at the same time giving both hands the
freedom to caress her. He caught her nipples between his
fingers and squeezed gently, smiling at the rippling cry of
pleasure he drew from her lips. The sight of her rose-tipped,
creamy curves nestled in his darker hands made fire pool
urgently in his body, swelling him against his jeans until he
could count each heartbeat as a separate surge of blood. He
caressed her hard nipples again, wishing he could take the
responsive flesh into his mouth.

Diana's breath fragmented into a low cry as Ten tugged rhythmically on her breasts, soothing and teasing her in the same skilled motions. He squeezed again, harder, knowing that she was now too aroused to feel a lighter touch. Her back arched in a passionate reflex that pressed her breasts against his hands. He rubbed slowly in return and was rewarded by a shivering cry of pleasure.

Deliberately Ten's hands retreated from Diana's breasts to her ribs, dragging slowly across her body, peeling away her bra and blouse. She made no objection, simply moved her shoulders sinuously, helping him. Her reward was the return of his hands to her breasts in a slow loving that drew ragged sighs from her lips; and then she felt the heat of his mouth going down her spine in a sensual glide that made her shiver repeatedly. Each restrained bite was a separate burst of pleasure sending glittering needles of sensation throughout her body. When his tongue traced her spine all the way up to her nape, she called out his name in a throaty voice she didn't recognize as her own.

"I'm right here, baby," Ten said, biting Diana's nape with enough force to leave small marks, tugging at the full breasts that lay within his cupped hands. "And so are you."

Slowly Ten released one breast and sent his hand down the front of her body again. "There is so much of you to enjoy," he said in a low voice. This time he didn't turn aside from the soft mound at the apex of her thighs. Nor did he linger. "Not just the obvious places, the battlegrounds of school kids," Ten continued, smoothing his hand over Diana's hip to the small of her back. "I like touching the rest of you, too." He traced the swell of her hip down to the back of her thighs, and from there to her firm calves and delicate ankles. "Smooth, firm . . ."

Ten's hand caressed higher, finding and stroking the inside of Diana's thighs as far as he could without seeming to pressure her for more than she was willing to give. His caress went from the back of her knee to the small of her back. He stroked first one hip, then the other, cupping and squeezing, drawing a surprised gasp of pleasure from her. She shifted almost restlessly, giving Ten's hand greater freedom. He moved his hand farther down, curling around her, holding her intimately. Heat burst through her, changing her gasp to a moan.

"Would you like lying just as you are now, but with no clothes to dull your pleasure?" Ten asked softly, kissing Diana's nape, her shoulder, her vulnerable spine. His hand tightened against her, subtly caressing her. "It's your choice, honey. You're as safe as you want to be."

"That's not...fair." The last word came out in a rippling sigh as Ten's hand flexed once more against her softness and heat.

"I thought you liked being teased," Ten said, smiling against Diana's spine despite the sudden, savage clenching of his own need.

"You're not teasing me," she whispered.

"I'm not?" Ten's hand flexed again and he groaned quietly at Diana's helpless response to his touch. "Baby, I'm sure as hell teasing one of us."

He felt her hand moving, heard the soft slide of a zipper and sensed the sudden looseness of her shorts. His hand bunched, catching cloth between his fingers, pulling it away from the hot secrets he longed to explore.

When Diana felt her remaining clothes being tugged down her legs, felt the powerful, cloth-covered male legs rubbing against hers, a shaft of panic went through her, memories of another time, another place, pain. Her legs clamped together and her body jackknifed in an instinctive effort to protect herself.

Instantly Ten let go, leaving Diana's shorts and panties around her knees. Grateful that she couldn't see the tension in his body, Ten brushed a butterfly kiss on her shoulder.

"It's all right, Diana. It stops right here."

Gently Ten began to ease his left arm from beneath Diana's head. She grabbed his left hand and held it against her breast once more.

"Don't leave," she said raggedly. "I didn't mean to react like that. It was just when I felt the zipper scrape down my leg and felt your legs and you were still dressed—but it's all right now. I know where I am, who I'm with."

Ten kissed Diana's shoulder again but made no move to reclaim the soft curves he had already made his own, much less the shadowed heat that lay newly revealed to his touch.

"Would it make you feel better if I weren't wearing my jeans?" Ten asked.

She laughed a little wildly. "Yes. I know it sounds crazy but—yes."

With a silent prayer that his self-control was as good as he thought it was, Ten rolled over, removed his clothes and returned to his former spoon position with Diana. The feel of her bare bottom nestled deeply into his lap made him clench against a savage thrust of need.

Diana and I could be dead naked together and she could still say no and that would be that. So cool off, cowboy. This one is for Diana, not me. As much as she wants, when she wants it, however she wants it. That's what I promised.

I must have been out of my mind.

The sweet heat and feminine curves of Diana's body called out to Ten in a siren song as old as man and woman and desire, making Ten want to curse his stupidity for promising not to coax or beg or demand from Diana what he had never needed so much before in his life.

He lay motionless, his left arm pillowing Diana's head, his right hand clenched into a fist that rested on his equally clenched thigh.

"Ten," Diana whispered. "Please touch me again. It's all right. I trust you. I won't panic again. And I like—I like the feel of you without your jeans."

Slowly Ten's right hand loosened. He took a deep, secret breath, then another, relaxing himself in a ritual that was almost as old as desire itself.

"Are you sure?" he asked, not knowing of whom he asked the question.

Diana answered it for both of them. Without warning she took both of Ten's hands and rubbed her breasts against his palms, letting him feel the hardness of her nipples and at the same time easing some of the wild ache in her body. His strong fingers closed around her, plucking at the tight velvet peaks, coaxing a ripple of sound from her. After a moment the smooth heat of his right hand caressed her belly, her waist, the small of her back; then a single finger traced the shadow cleft between her hips.

If Diana had thought to conceal herself by locking her knees together and jackknifing her body, she had failed. Ten found her softness unshielded, defenseless, and he traced it lovingly. A sudden shudder took her whole body, surprising her. Her husky cry was matched by Ten's groan of discovery as her heat and pleasure spilled over him.

"Ten," Diana cried, feeling another of the strange, tiny convulsions building in her. "I—"

The word became a gasp and another shudder and then another as she felt his touch glide into her body, retreat, return, only to retreat once more, leaving her dazed and empty, aching. He skimmed the edges of her softness, probing sweetly, discovering the aching nub hidden between sleek, silken folds, rubbing it slowly, hotly, stripping away her breath, her thoughts, her restraint.

Diana twisted sinuously, trying to know more of the pleasure that was greater than any she had ever felt but still not enough; it was driving her mad. *Ten* was driving her mad, stealing into her so gently, retreating, always retreating when what she wanted, what she must have, was his own flesh filling the emptiness she had never known existed within her own body.

"So soft," Ten said, his deep voice a rumbling purr. He teased Diana slowly, loving the wild tremors of her response when he slid unerringly into her softness, groaning as he touched as much of her as he could. "So damned hot."

Ten's name broke on Diana's lips, a strained sound that could have been either fear or passion. Slowly, reluctantly, he began withdrawing from her body. Her hand locked over his, holding him in place.

"Are you sure you want this?" Ten said hoarsely, rubbing his cheek along her bare hip.

"Yes."

"And this? Do you want this, too?"

His hand shifted. The sensuous pressure within Diana increased. The glittering sensation that had haunted her body condensed into a network of wild lightning. The sound she made was as involuntary as the tightening of her body around him. Afraid that he had hurt her, Ten withdrew before she could stop him.

"Baby? Was that pleasure or pain? You're so tight..."

Diana looked over her shoulder at Ten with sapphire eyes that burned in the aftermath of sensual lightning. Slowly she turned her whole body until she was facing him. When she spoke, her voice was low, smoky, as helplessly sensual as her response to him. She guided his hand from her shoulder to the dark triangle at the base of her torso. When he accepted her wordless invitation and returned to her body, a shaft of pleasure made her gasp and tremble even as she instinctively sought more of Ten's touch. His hand shifted and she felt herself gently stretched. Sensual lightning came again, as unexpected and ravishing as it had been the first time.

"You were right," Diana said when she could speak.

"About what?"

"This. It's as much pleasure as your senses can stand."

Ten laughed softly, then groaned as Diana's mouth caressed his bare chest. "We've just skimmed the surface," he said, bringing her mouth up to his. "But I'm glad you're enjoying it."

She smiled hesitantly. "Are you enjoying it, too?"

"Baby, I'd have to be dead and buried not to enjoy touching you."

Ten felt Diana's slender fingers searching restlessly over his chest, pausing to tease the flat male nipples, then moving on to his back. She probed the line of his spine between ridges of muscle, stroking him, learning what it felt like to hold a man in her arms. Closing her eyes, sighing, half-smiling, she kneaded the long, heavy muscles of Ten's back, openly savoring the heat and power of his body.

Seeing Diana's enjoyment at touching him was as arousing as anything a woman had ever done to Ten. The tips of Diana's breasts were like tight pink rosebuds pressing against him with each movement of her hands. When he could no longer bear looking at her breasts without caressing them, he bent his head to her. A startled gasp became a moan as he circled one bud with his tongue, then took her deeply into his mouth, tasting her, tugging softly on her, making her shudder with each soft stab of his tongue, each exquisitely restrained caress of his teeth, each movement of his fingers within the clinging heat of her body.

Sounds rippled from Diana, the elemental huskiness of passion combined with rising notes of feminine surprise. The hot movements of Ten's mouth and hands increased, deepened, quickened, and she called his name with every rapid breath she took, every stroke of sweet lightning scoring her, shaking her, until finally she shimmered and burned in his arms, her body consumed by the pleasure he had given to her.

Ten held Diana as close as he dared, stroking her trembling body with hands that also trembled, kissing her flushed cheeks, her eyelids, her reddened lips, until finally her breath came more evenly. Her lashes stirred and lifted, revealing eyes more blue than any gems Ten had ever seen.

"How can I . . . what do I say?" Diana whispered.

"Whatever you want."

"I love you, Ten."

The line of Ten's lips shifted into a bittersweet smile. Before she could say any more, he kissed her gently. "I'm glad you enjoyed it, baby. Damned glad."

Diana opened her mouth to object that what she felt was more than the aftermath of physical pleasure, but Ten's tongue slid between her lips. Without thinking she closed her teeth, lightly raking his tongue, then soothing it with slow motions of her own in a pattern he had taught her. The tightening of his body in response and the sweet friction of his own tongue made her nerve endings shimmer again, echoes of lightning from her breasts to her knees. Her breath caught, broke, caught again.

"Ten?"

He closed his eyes, trying to ignore both the soft heat of Diana's body and the hard heat of his own.

"I want more of you," Diana said huskily, sweeping her hands from his shoulders to his waist. "I want all of you. If you—do you want me, too?"

"Move your hands down a little more and tell me what you think," Ten said hoarsely.

She had moved her hands barely at all when she discovered precisely what he meant. The sound he made while she measured his arousal with a slow pressure of her palm could have been pain, but she was looking at his eyes and she knew it wasn't. She repeated the caress again, drawing another hoarse, low sound.

"Baby, you'll . . ."

Ten's breath hissed between his clenched teeth. His hand slid from Diana's knee to the apex of her thighs as he sought the secret well of her femininity. It was even hotter and softer than his memories. She whimpered and moved with his touch. Her response and her hands searching over his hard, eager flesh nearly undid him.

Very carefully Ten eased Diana's hands up his body, kissed her fingertips and palms and held them hard against his chest while he caught his breath.

"Ten? What's wrong?"

"Hush, baby. Nothing's wrong."

Ten turned away and took a packet from his jeans pocket. With the swift, sure motions of a man performing an accustomed task, he opened the packet. When he turned back to Diana he wasn't completely naked. He saw her rather startled, somewhat dismayed look. With a calm that was exactly opposite to what he was feeling, he put his finger under her chin and tilted her face up to his own.

"Want to change your mind?" Ten asked.

Rather tentatively, Diana ran her fingertips over Ten's tightly sheathed flesh. "It felt better... without."

He clenched his teeth against agreeing with her. It had felt one hell of a lot better to be completely naked. Just as she, now, felt exquisite to his bare fingers as he once more slid into her, testing her readiness to receive him and simultaneously drawing a low sound of pleasure from her as she melted at his touch.

"Sex is temporary," Ten said tightly. "Children aren't. It's a small price to pay for a big amount of protection."

Diana's head snapped up, surprise clear on her face. At that moment Ten realized she hadn't even considered the fact that she might become pregnant. He wanted to swear and laugh and then swear some more at her trust, but most of all he wanted to plumb the depths of her heat with the very flesh that she was once again caressing tentatively. Though her touch was muffled by the price of protecting himself against the lifetime complications of fatherhood, the feel of her hand was nonetheless driving him to the edge of his control.

"Baby?" Ten said.

The aching restraint in his voice made Diana's heart turn over. "Yes," she whispered. "Whatever you want, just show me."

"The first time, it would be easier if . . . will it bother you to be beneath me?"

"No."

"Are you sure?"

Holding Ten's eyes with her own, Diana lay back and opened herself to him. Her complete trust pierced Ten, making him tremble with an emotion that was deeper and more devastating than desire. Slowly he settled between her legs, watching her for any sign of fear or pain. He saw only blue eyes that widened slightly at the gently probing pressure between her legs, then her eyes closed and she unraveled in a long, shivering acceptance of him within her body.

The ease with which Ten became a part of Diana was another instant of piercing emotion deep within him . . . and then he was moving and she was clinging to him, measuring him in a new way, moving with him, loving him as she had never loved another man.

Fire swept through Ten's restraint, burning him, burning her, each wanting more and yet more. Instinctively Diana's legs shifted, wrapping around his lean hips, luring and demanding with the same motions. He answered with hard, sweeping movements, driving into her, filling her, drinking from her sweet mouth until he felt his self-control slipping away. He fought against ecstasy, not wanting it to come to him so soon, not wanting to end the burning arousal that was in itself a savage pleasure; then it was too late, the pleasure was too piercing, too overwhelming.

Ten took her one final time, all of her, and held himself there while ecstasy stripped everything away but Diana and the deep, endless pulses of his own release.

Fourteen

———

Ten sat in the rocking chair, moving it with a gentle rhythm, looking down into Logan's turquoise eyes. The baby stared with absolute seriousness back into Ten's eyes.

"I know, old man," Ten said, smiling. "I don't look like your momma. What's worse, I'm not built like her and you're getting too hungry to be pacified by a rocking chair and a soothing voice much longer. But I'm afraid you'll just have to lump it for a while. Luke has been trying to show Carla that new colt all day, and this is the first chance they've had. You don't begrudge your parents a few minutes alone together, do you?"

Ten smiled to himself as he spoke. He suspected the new colt wasn't all that was keeping Luke and Carla away from the house. The men were scattered all over the ranch, Diana was working on sketches at the old house, Ten had promised to watch Logan, and the barn was empty of all but a few horses. Ten wouldn't have blamed Luke for taking advantage of the opportunity to steal a few kisses or even the whole woman.

The thought of enjoying a similar opportunity to have Diana alone within the twilight silence of the barn had a rapid and very pronounced effect on Ten's body.

"Damn," he muttered softly. "It's not like I've been exactly deprived in that department, except for the weekends."

When they were away from September Canyon, Ten was careful not to show any difference in his treatment of Diana. Some women could have laughed off or ignored the cowhands' brand of humor with regard to "unwed marriage" or "riding double" or the like, but Ten didn't think Diana was one of them. When the hands discovered, as they quickly would, that no marriage was planned, the humor would degenerate into sidelong looks and blunt male speculations. Diana's trust and uninhibited sensuality deserved better than that. She was very different from the kind of women the cowboys associated with summer flings.

The only time Ten allowed himself to be alone with Diana was in the old house, in the workroom, sorting shards after dinner, the curtains open and both people plainly in view to anyone who cared enough to glance in. Outwardly, as long as anyone was around, nothing had changed since Diana had become his lover.

As much as Ten was tempted by proximity, he didn't so much as kiss Diana when they were at the ranch house. He didn't trust himself to stop with a kiss or two. On Friday, the drive back from September Canyon had taken so long that dinner was over hours before Ten and Diana made it to the ranch house. Part of the trouble had been a rain-slicked road. The other part had been Diana; Ten hadn't been able to keep his hands off her. What had started as a quick kiss had ended with both of them breathing too hard, too fast, their breath as steamy as their bodies had become.

All that had prevented Ten from taking Diana right there was the fact that her first, unhappy experience with sex had been in the front seat of a vehicle. So he had put the truck back in gear and driven to the ranch with the weekend stretching like eternity in front of him. But it had been a near thing. He had never been like that with a woman, riding the eroding edge of his own self-control until he wanted to put his fist through a window in sheer frustration.

Two nights in the bunkhouse did nothing to make him feel better. No matter how hard Ten tried not to, he kept seeing Diana holding out her arms, opening herself to him. The memory made heat and heaviness pool thickly between his thighs, a reaction that had become uncomfortably familiar since he had first seen Diana.

Becoming her lover had meant only a temporary improvement in the condition, followed all too soon by an even more pronounced return of the problem. Knowing the passion that lay behind Diana's smile didn't help to cool Ten's response. He wanted to make love to her after an evening of conversation and laughter, and then again in the middle of the night, and then he wanted to kiss her slowly awake in the morning, bringing her from dreams to passion, watching the pleasure in her eyes when she woke up and found him inside her. But he couldn't do that on the weekends, when they returned to the ranch house.

Logan bunched up his little fists and cried.

Ten sighed. "I know how you feel, nubbin. I know how you feel."

He shifted the baby and stroked the tiny cheek with his fingertip. Logan's hands flailed with excitement until more by chance than anything else he connected with Ten's left index finger, bringing it to his mouth. Instantly the baby began sucking on Ten's callused fingertip.

"Uh, old man, I don't know how to break this to you, but . . . oh, the hell with it. You'll figure it out for yourself soon enough."

The controlled, throaty rumble of a powerful car engine distracted Ten. He looked out through the window into the last light of evening. The paint job on the car was a dirt-streaked, sun-faded black, but everything that affected the car's function was in top shape. The tires were new, the lights were bright and hard, and the engine purred like a well-fed cougar.

Even before the driver got out and stretched, Ten knew that Nevada Blackthorn had come back to the Rocking M.

Smiling with anticipation, Ten watched his younger brother climb the front steps with the lithe, coordinated motions of an athlete or a highly trained warrior. The knock on the door was distinct, staccato without being impatient. Ten's smile widened. There had been a time when his brother would have driven up in a cloud of dust and knocked on the door hard enough to rattle the hinges.

"Come on in, Nevada."

The door opened and shut without noise. Nevada crossed the room the same way. Without noise. Tall, wide-shouldered, his thick black hair two inches long and his dense beard half that length, Nevada looked as hard as he was. Even as his pale, ice-green eyes took in the room with its multiple doorways, his unnaturally acute hearing noted the near-silent approach of someone coming toward the living room through the kitchen.

Knowing that Ten was baby-sitting Logan, Diana had been all but tiptoeing across the kitchen as she headed for the living room. She didn't get that far. Two steps from the doorway she froze at the sight of the lean, long-boned, broad-shouldered stranger who moved like Ten when he was fighting.

Ten held Logan and watched Nevada cross the floor toward the rocking chair. Rain-colored eyes measured the changes in Nevada—the brackets of anger or pain around his flat, unsmiling mouth, the razor-fine physical edge, his muscular weight always poised on the balls of his feet because he had to be ready to throw himself into flight or battle at every instant. For Ten, looking at Nevada was like going back in time, seeing himself years ago, youthful dreams and emotions burned out by the timeless cruelty of war.

Silently Nevada stood in front of the rocking chair, staring down at his brother and the baby.

"I will be damned. Yours?"

Ten shook his head. "Not a chance. I know what kind of husband I make. I'm definitely a short-term man. Marriage should be a long-term affair."

Nevada grunted. "The bitch you married didn't make much of a wife, long or short."

The corner of Ten's mouth curled sardonically. "It wasn't all her fault. Women aren't interested in me for more than a few weeks."

"The way I remember it, you weren't real interested yourself after a few weeks. Two months was your limit. Then you were tugging at the bit, looking for new worlds to conquer."

"The curse of the Blackthorns," Ten agreed, his voice casual. "Warriors, not husbands."

Diana stood motionless, her throat clenched around a cry of protest and pain, realizing that she had lost a gamble she hadn't even understood she was taking. She had understood the risk of physical injury she took in trusting Ten, and she had been lucky; Ten had given her extraordinary physical pleasure and no pain at all.

But she hadn't understood that she was risking her emotions and unborn dreams. Now she felt as she had the instant the kiva ceiling had given way beneath her feet.

No wonder Ten has been so careful not to touch me when other people are around. He doesn't want them to know we're lovers. They might assume something more, something that has to do with shared lives, shared promises, shared love. But he doesn't see us that way.

I didn't know I saw us that way until now, just now, when a dream I didn't even know I had burst and I fell through to reality.

God, I hope the landing is easier than the fall.

Diana clenched her teeth and forced herself to let out the breath she had instinctively held at the first instant of tearing pain. Silently, gradually, she took in air and let it out again, bringing strength back to her body. After a few aching breaths, her ears stopped ringing. The words from the other room began to have meaning again, Nevada speaking in tones that were like Ten's but without the emotion.

"Heard anything from Utah?"

"He's tired of jungles," Ten said.

Nevada grunted. "Anytime he wants to swap sea-level tropics for Afghanistan's high passes, he can have at it."

"Thought the country calmed down after the Russians left." Ten gave Nevada a measuring, gray-eyed glance. "Thought that was why you decided to come home."

"The Afghani tribesmen have been killing each other for a thousand years. They'll be killing each other a thousand years from now. They're fighting men. They'd take on Satan for the pure hell of it."

"So would you."

Nevada's pale green eyes locked with Ten's. "I did. I lost."

Ten held out his right hand. "I don't know of any man who ever won. Welcome back, brother. You've been a long time coming home."

The deep affection in Ten's voice went through Diana, shaking her all over again, telling her that she was jealous of Ten's brother. The realization appalled her, and the pain.

All the old wives' tales are true: the landing is worse than the fall.

Diana looked around almost wildly. She had to leave, and leave quickly, before she was discovered. She couldn't face Ten with jealousy and despair and pain shaking her.

"Never thought I'd say it," Nevada said quietly, "but it's good to see your ugly face again. Now maybe you'll introduce me to the lady standing behind me."

Ten leaned sideways, looking around his brother's body toward the front door.

"Kitchen door," Nevada said, stepping aside.

Diana heard the words but took another step backward anyway, wondering bitterly how Nevada had known she was behind him. She hadn't made a sound. In fact, she had barely breathed, especially after hearing Ten's matter-of-fact summation of his lack of enduring appeal to women.

And theirs to him.

"Diana? Is that you? Come on in, honey. I want you to meet my brother Nevada. Nevada, this is Diana Saxton."

Nevada turned around and Diana knew she couldn't flee. The pale green eyes that were examining her were as passionless as Nevada's voice. She had an unnerving sense of looking into the eyes of a wolf or a cougar.

"How did you know I was here?" Diana asked almost angrily.

"Your scent."

Nevada's neutral tone did nothing to calm Diana. The man's unsmiling, measuring aloofness overwhelmed all other impressions she had of him, even the obvious one of his dark, hard, male appeal.

Nevada looked from Diana to the baby sucking industriously on Ten's finger. "Yours?"

"No," she said in a strained voice. "That's Logan MacKenzie."

"Luke's baby?" Nevada asked, looking at Ten.

Ten nodded.

"You mean that long-legged little girl you told me about finally ran him to ground?"

"She sure did. Then she let him go. He decided he didn't want to go anywhere without her."

Nevada shrugged. "To each his own. For the Blackthorns, that means single harness, not double."

Ten looked at Diana's tight, pale face and at his brother, who was a younger, harder reflection of himself. Ten looked down for a long moment at the baby in his lap, then he met again the unsmiling eyes of a warrior who had fought too long.

"Hope you haven't lost your taste for sleeping out," Ten said. "Jervis is getting damned tired of weekends in September Canyon."

"I don't sleep much, so it doesn't matter where I lie down."

Ten's eyes narrowed as he remembered the years he had spent relearning how to sleep like a civilized man instead of a wild animal, coming alert with every unusual noise, waking up in a single rush with a knife in one hand and a man's throat in the other.

"It will pass," Ten said quietly.

Nevada said nothing.

Logan began to fret, no longer pacified by Ten's unyielding fingertip.

Nevada watched the baby for a moment, then said, "Company coming from the barn. Man and a woman."

Ten shook his head at the acuity of Nevada's senses. "I'm glad I don't have to live like that anymore, every sense peeled to maximum alertness."

"Beats dying."

The very faint sound of a woman's laughter floated into the living room. Logan's fretfulness increased in volume.

"Honey," Ten said to Diana without looking away from the baby, "go tell Carla to get a move on it. Logan is getting set to cloud up and rain all over me."

There was no answer. Ten glanced up from Logan's rapidly reddening face. Diana was gone.

"How long was she standing there?" Ten said, his voice as hard as Nevada's.

"Long enough to know you're not interested in marrying her."

Ten closed his eyes and hissed a single, savage word. It would be a long drive to September Canyon tomorrow, and all the way Diana would be tight, angry, thinking of a thousand reasons why she shouldn't melt and run like hot, wild honey at his touch.

Logan began to cry in earnest, gulping in air and letting it out in jerky squalls.

"That's a strong baby you have there," Nevada said. He bent down. A long, scarred finger traced Logan's hairline with surprising delicacy. "It's good to hear a baby cry and know its distress is only temporary, that food and love are on the way."

"Less volume would be nice."

Nevada shook his head and said in a low voice, "The ones who are too weak to cry are the hardest to take."

Ten looked up quickly. His brother's eyes were hooded, unreadable. The front door opened and Carla rushed in.

"I'm sorry, I thought Logan would be all right for a few more minutes." She saw Nevada, noted the similarity to Ten in build and stance and smiled. "Nevada Blackthorn, right?" she asked, reaching past the bearded man for her hollering baby. "I'm Carla. Welcome to the Rocking M. We've never met but I've heard a lot about you." As she hurried from the room with Logan in her arms, she called over her shoulder, "Luke, look who finally got here. Now Jervis can go back to chasing cows."

Soon after Carla disappeared into the next room, the sound of the baby's crying ended abruptly, telling the men that Logan had found something more satisfactory to suckle than a man's calloused fingertip.

Luke shut the door and walked across the living room. For a few seconds there was silence while Nevada and Luke measured each other. Then Luke nodded and held out his hand.

"Welcome back, Nevada. The Rocking M is your home for as long as you want it."

After a moment Nevada took the hand that was offered. "Thanks, MacKenzie. You won't regret it."

Luke turned to Ten, measured the expression on his face and asked rather warily, "Something wrong, ramrod?"

"Not one damn thing." Ten stood and crossed the room in long strides. "Come on, Nevada. I'll show you where you'll be sleeping."

The front door closed behind Ten.

Luke looked questioningly at Nevada.

"Woman trouble," Nevada said succinctly.

"What?"

"Five foot three, blue eyes, a fine body she tries to hide underneath a man's sweater."

"Diana?"

Nevada nodded.

"Did you say Ten's *woman?*"

Nevada shrugged. "She will be until she tries to put a permanent brand on him. Then she'll be looking for another stud to ride. Blackthorns don't brand worth a damn."

Fifteen

Ten was right about the length of the drive to September Canyon. And the silence. Diana slept most of the way despite the roughness of the road, telling Ten two things. The first was that she trusted his driving skills, but he already knew that. The second was that she must have slept damned little the night before to be able to sleep so soundly now in the rolling front seat of the pickup truck.

When Ten could take it no longer, he said, "Diana."

Her eyes opened. They were dark, clear, and their color was an indigo as bottomless as twilight.

"Pounce's purring must have kept you up all night," Ten said, watching the road. One look at Diana's eyes had been enough.

"Pounce hunts at night." The thought of the cat gliding through darkness in search of prey reminded Diana of Nevada. "Like Nevada."

"He lived as a warrior too long. Like me. And like me, Nevada will heal," Ten said matter-of-factly. "It just takes time."

Diana made a sound that could have meant anything.

Ten waited.

No more sounds came from the other side of the truck.

"I was glad to see that Nevada and Luke didn't have to sort things out the hard way," Ten continued. "They'll get along fine now that life has knocked some sense into both of their hard heads."

Diana said nothing.

With a hunger Ten wasn't aware of, he watched her for a few instants before the road claimed his attention again. Telling himself to be patient, he waited for her to speak. And he waited.

And waited.

Ten was still waiting when they forded Picture Wash and bumped up September Canyon to the overhang. It wasn't the first time he and Diana had gone for hours without conversation, but it was the first time the silence hadn't been comfortable. Getting out of the truck didn't increase Diana's desire to talk. They unloaded supplies with a minimum of words, each doing his or her accustomed part around the camp.

Without a word Ten carried the two bedrolls to the edge of the overhang, dragged two camp mattresses over and began making up the single, oversize bedroll he and Diana would share. He sensed her watching him, but she said nothing. When he straightened and looked around, he saw Diana shrugging into her backpack, clearly preparing to go out and sketch in the rapidly failing light. His arm shot out and his fingers curled hard around her wrist.

"Dammit!" Ten said. "You were the one who came to me! I never promised you anything!"

Diana's eyes were wide and dark against her pale face. For a long, stretching moment she looked at Ten, letting the truth echo around her like thunder while painful lightning searched through her body and soul.

"Yes," she said huskily. "I know."

Ten's hands tightened. Her agreement should have made him feel better, but it didn't. He kept remembering the moment when she had looked at him with eyes still dazed by her first taste of sexual pleasure and whispered that she loved him.

Now her eyes were filled with pain. He had never felt another person's pain so clearly, as clearly as his own.

"Listen to me," Ten said roughly. "The pleasure you feel when we have sex—that isn't love. It will wear off. It always does. But until it does, there's no reason you shouldn't enjoy it to the fullest."

The slight flinching of Diana's eyelids was the only betrayal of her emotions. "That's very kind of you, Tennessee."

Her soft, even voice scored Ten like a whip.

"*Kind?* I'm not some damn charity worker. I'm a man and I enjoy sex with you a hell of a lot more than I've ever enjoyed it with any woman. What we have in bed is damned rare and I know it even if you don't!"

Diana looked up into the blazing clarity of Ten's eyes. She didn't doubt that he meant exactly what he had said. She drew a deep breath, drinking his complex truth to the last bittersweet drop. Pleasure, not love. But a rare pleasure, one he valued.

"I'm glad," she said finally.

And that, too, was a complex, bittersweet truth.

Ten should have been relieved at Diana's acknowledgment that what they shared in bed wasn't love. But he wasn't relieved. She understood, she agreed—and somehow she had never been farther away from him, even the first day when she had turned and run from him.

Swearing beneath his breath, Ten stood with his fingers locked around Diana's wrist and wondered savagely how he and she could be so painfully honest with each other and yet somehow allow an important truth to slide through their fingers like rain through sand, sinking down and down and down, farther out of reach with every second.

"To hell with talking," he said savagely.

Ten bent his arm, bringing Diana hard against his body. His tongue searched the surprised softness of her mouth with urgent movements. The hunger that had been just beneath his surface blazed up, shortening his breath, making his blood run heavily, hardening his body in a rushing instant that he felt all the way to his heels; but Diana was stiff in his arms, vibrating with emotions that had little to do with desire.

"Don't fight me, baby," Ten said heavily against Diana's mouth, his voice as dark and hot as his kiss had been. "What we have is too rare and too good to waste on anger."

Ten probed the center of Diana's ear with the hot tip of his tongue, feeling her shiver helplessly in response. He probed again and was rewarded by another sensuous shiver. With a low sound of triumph, he caught the rim of her ear between his teeth and bit delicately, repeatedly, demanding and also pleading for her response.

The intensity and need within Ten reached past Diana's pain to the love beneath. She tried to speak, didn't trust her uncertain hold on her emotions and slid her arms around Ten's lean waist instead. His breath came out in a barely audible sigh of relief when he felt her soften against him.

"Diana," Ten whispered, hugging her in return, "baby, I don't want to hurt you. When you gave yourself to me that first time, looking right at me, knowing to the last quarter inch how much I wanted you . . ." Memory lanced through Ten, making him shudder. "Yet you held out your arms to me. No one has ever trusted me like that. I was so afraid of hurting you I almost didn't go through with it."

She looked at him with startled blue eyes.

"It's true," Ten said, easing his fingers into Diana's cool, soft hair. "I was arguing with myself all the way down into your arms. Then you took me so perfectly and I knew I wouldn't hurt you. Your body was made for mine. And somehow you knew it, too, didn't you? That's why you watched me with such curiosity and hunger, day after day, until I thought I would go crazy. Then you asked me to kiss you and I was sure I would go crazy. You fit my hands perfectly, my arms, my mouth, my body. I knew it was going to be so damned *good.* I was right. It was good then and it's even better now, each time better than the last."

The words caressed Diana even more than the heat of Ten's body or the pressure of his fingers rubbing slowly down her spine.

"Is it that way for you, too?" Ten asked. "Tell me it's that way for you, too."

He bent to kiss Diana's neck with barely restrained force, arching her against his body, letting her feel his strength and what she had done to him.

"Baby?"

"Yes," she said as she gave herself to his power. "You must know it is, Ten. Don't you know?"

"I do now," he whispered against her hair, and then he whispered it again.

Slowly Ten straightened. He held Diana gently against his chest, just held her, as though he were afraid to ask for any more than she had already given.

And he was.

"Go ahead and sketch while you still have light," Ten said finally, kissing Diana's eyelids, brushing his lips gently across her mouth, caresses without demand. "I'll open the new box of shards and see what the grads found over the weekend."

Shaking, feeling like crying in protest when Ten turned away, hungry for him in a way that eclipsed anything she had ever felt before, Diana looked blindly out over September Canyon. She couldn't force herself to walk away from the overhang and the man she loved more with every day.

And with every day she was closer to losing him.

The pleasure you feel when we have sex—that isn't love. It will wear off. It always does.

But it wouldn't for her. Diana knew that as surely as she had known she could trust Ten not to force anything more from her than she wanted to give. She had been right. He had taken nothing from her that she hadn't given willingly.

It wasn't Ten's fault that he didn't want everything she had to give to a man.

Though Diana knew sketching would be impossible, she took off her backpack, brought out her pad, opened it and sat down on the bedroll she would share that night with Ten. Adrift on the cool wind flowing down from the mesa top, she looked out over the canyon she loved. She saw neither trees nor cliffs nor even the wild beauty of the setting sun, only the image of the man she had come to love even more than the land.

In her mind she saw Ten's face with eerie precision, each line that sun and wind had etched around his eyes, eyes whose probing clarity had first unnerved, then fascinated her. The same was true of Ten's powerful, unmistakably male body; first it had frightened and then finally it had fascinated her.

Now, in the clear light of pain, Diana acknowledged what she had previously been too caught up within her own fears and needs to see—the shadows that lay beneath the clarity of Ten's eyes, the reserve that lay beneath his passion, the internal walls he had built as carefully as an Anasazi cliff fortress, walls keeping her out, his own words describing solitude.

He lived as a warrior too long. Like me. And like me, Nevada will heal. It just takes time.

But Ten hadn't healed. Not wholly.

She wanted to heal him. She needed to. But there were so few weeks left to remove scars that were years deep, a wounding so old, so accustomed a part of the man she loved, that Ten himself didn't even realize that he hadn't healed. He had scarred over, which wasn't the same thing at all.

"Such a pensive look," Ten said. Sitting down next to Diana, he glanced at the drawing in her lap. It was a close-up of September Canyon's ruins, detailing the precarious eyelash of a trail that led from the cliff dwellings up the face of the cliff to the mesa above. "Are you thinking about the Anasazi again, trapped within their own creation?"

"And time," Diana said, her voice husky, aching as she flipped slowly through the sketchbook. "Time is another kind of trap."

"Why? Are you getting behind in your sketching?"

"No. I'll be finished well within the deadline."

"Deadline?"

"The middle of August. That's when my contract with the Rocking M ends."

Ten looked deeply into Diana's eyes, wanting to protest what lay beneath her quiet words: when the contract ended, she would leave the Rocking M and Tennessee Blackthorn.

Diana looked only at the sketch in her lap, praying that Ten would reach past the wall he had built and ask her to stay without the pretense of archaeological work between them.

Ask me to stay, Ten. Ask me as a man asks a woman he wants and needs and might someday love. Please, love, ask me.

Silently, Ten's fingertips traced the line of Diana's chin, tilting her face up to his lips. He kissed her slowly, seducing her mouth for long moments before accepting the invitation of her parted lips and warm tongue. With controlled urgency he began undressing her, only to discover that he was being undressed, as well. Relief coursed through him almost as violently as desire. He kissed her again, drinking deeply, urgently, from the woman who haunted his sleep even when she was lying by his side.

By the time the kiss ended, their breathing was ragged and their clothes were scattered randomly around the bedroll.

Ten's hand slid from Diana's ankle to the apex of her thighs. The deep, sultry welcome of her body made blood hammer in his veins until he could hardly breathe.

"It's a little soon to be mentally packing your gear, isn't it?" Ten asked in a low, rough voice as he caressed Diana, calling forth a husky moan and a tiny, searing melting. "A lot could happen in the next few weeks."

"Could it?" Diana asked, hope leaping even more hotly than desire within her body.

"Sure. The Rocking M is going to need some expert advice on excavating the kiva you discovered. Who better than you to give it?"

Before Diana could speak, Ten took her mouth. The slowly building pressure of his kiss arched her across his hard forearm. She gave herself to the kiss and to the man, feeling desire and regret, caring and hunger, passion and restraint in Ten's embrace, every emotion except the love that filled her until she ached.

When the long kiss ended, Ten lifted his mouth with tangible reluctance.

"There's no reason not to extend your contract."

"Luke might see it differently."

"September Canyon is my land. The dig is being underwritten by my money. If I want it to go beyond the middle of August, it will."

Diana shuddered from desire and grief mixed together, feeling as though she had been turned inside out until everything she was and could be lay exposed to the cool sunset light. Bittersweet understanding of the difference between her own needs and Ten's knifed through her, and in its wake an anguished acceptance.

She wanted his laughter, his grief, his victories, his defeats, his silence, his conversations. She wanted his body, his mind, his children and a lifetime of tomorrows. He wanted the passion that ran like invisible lightning between them, and he wanted every bit of it for as long as it lasted.

She loved him. He did not love her. But she could take from him one of the things she wanted and give him the only thing he wanted in return.

Diana rolled onto her side and began running her hands down Ten's muscular torso, caressing and inciting him with the same motions.

"No, there's no reason at all not to extend the contract," Diana said, finding and teasing a flat male nipple with her teeth, "except common sense."

"What does that mean?"

"Simple. As simple as this."

Her hands closed around the thick evidence of Ten's desire and he groaned with leaping need. She continued talking as she caressed the length of his body, scattering his thoughts, taking away everything but the heat of her mouth.

"The Rocking M—" Diana's tongue probed Ten's navel "—can't afford to pay me." She closed her teeth on the tightly flexed muscles that joined neck and shoulder. A shudder moved the length of his body. "Not as much as I earn being an assistant professor at the university."

"We could—work something out. Weekends. Vacations." Ten's breath came in with a hissing sound as Diana nuzzled his ear, teasing, biting. "Part-time work. Something."

Diana's eyes closed against a wave of pain, but her mouth and hands remained gentle, loving Ten, sharing with and returning to him the gift of passion he had given so generously to her. After a few moments she could trust herself to speak again.

"You don't have to pay me to come to the Rocking M." She bit the hard muscle of Ten's biceps in a sensual punishment that was just short of pain. "All you have to do is ask. Or you can come to Boulder when you feel like it."

"Diana..."

She waited, hope penned within her acceptance like a wild animal.

Ten made a half-angry, half-helpless sound.

She let out her breath in a long, soundless sigh, knowing acceptance had been right and hope had been wrong.

"I agree," Diana said softly. "It's better to keep it just a summer affair."

"That's not what I said."

"No. It's what you meant."

"Dammit," Ten said roughly, "I learned long ago that I'm piss-poor husband material."

"Did you?" Diana asked, lifting her head, looking into Ten's narrowed eyes. "Or did you just decide sex isn't worth all the inconvenience of marriage?"

Bleak gray eyes searched Diana's face.

Smiling sadly, she turned away and let her mouth slide down the warm, muscular tension of his abdomen. "It's all right, Tennessee. I learned something long ago, too. Then you came along and taught me that I hadn't learned everything."

Diana's cheek rested for a moment on a dense cushion of black, curly hair. Her lips brushed flesh that was hot, smooth, hard, pulsing with the swift beat of Ten's life. When she moved her head to test the resilience of his thigh with her teeth, Ten made a deep sound. When her head turned again and the tip of her tongue touched him curiously, his breath came out in a low groan that was also her name.

"If I made you a promise," Diana said, biting Ten lightly once more, stroking the thick muscles of his thighs, skimming over without ever really touching the hard, violently sensitive flesh that she had aroused, "would you trust me to keep it? Would you trust me not to ask you for anything more, ever?"

Blindly Ten reached for his jeans, his fingers seeking the familiar packet, finding it.

"Tennessee," Diana whispered, brushing her lips over the musky cushion of hair, touching his hot flesh with the tip of her tongue. "Do you trust my promise?"

He groaned as a fine sheen of passion broke over his skin. His right hand clenched, crumpling the packet. "Baby, it's damned hard to think when you're doing that."

"Then don't think. Just answer from the instinctive part of you. Do you trust me to keep my promise about never asking for one more thing from you?"

"Yes," Ten said hoarsely, knowing as he spoke that it was true. He could trust Diana's word. "What do you—want?"

"This."

The sound Ten made was a combination of surprise and searing pleasure as Diana's mouth tasted him with lingering sensual curiosity.

"When I first asked you to kiss me," she whispered against his hot skin, "it was because I wanted to be able to lead a normal life, and that meant responding to men the way other women did. And it worked, up to a point. But then I began trying to imagine other men touching me the way you had, and I knew I wouldn't be able to go through with it."

"Fear?" Ten asked, the only word he could force past the passionate constriction in his throat.

Diana shook her head. Tendrils of silky hair brushed over Ten's skin in the instant before her mouth circled him in a caress that took what little breath he had remaining, tasting him, loving him as she never had before. When the caress deepened, Ten's whole body flushed with wild heat. She held him for long moments, savoring him, loving the wildness coursing through him at her caress. Slowly, reluctantly, she released him from tender captivity.

She lifted her head and met the smoldering brilliance of Ten's eyes. The look in them made her body melt. He felt it, knew that she wanted him as wildly as he wanted her, and had to close his eyes against the force of the need twisting through his body.

"It's not fear that will keep me away from other men," Diana said finally, biting Ten with great gentleness, feeling the wave of desire that swept through him almost as clearly as he did. "It's the fact that I don't want them. Other men wouldn't have rain-colored eyes that blaze with desire. Other men wouldn't have a scar below their jawline or one on their shoulder, their hip, the inside of their left thigh. Other men wouldn't be able to handle a brute and a kitten with the same ease. Other men wouldn't look like you, feel like you . . . taste like you."

Ten made a hoarse sound of intense pleasure as the moist heat of Diana's mouth caressed him again. He called her name roughly, feeling the world being stripped away with each silky movement of her tongue.

"Make love without barriers for the weeks I have left on the Rocking M," she said. "Be completely naked inside me. No matter what happens afterward, there won't be any demands, any regrets." Slowly Diana slid up Ten's body until the thick length of his arousal skimmed her softness, making her breath break. "Ten?"

His own breath came in with a harsh, ripping sound as she melted over him. "I'm not sure I can hold back with you, baby," he said roughly. "You could get pregnant. Have you thought of that?"

"Yes," Diana said, shivering, melting, searing him with her need. "Many times."

Ten's right hand opened with a savage movement, sending the small packet tumbling onto the ground. He lay still but for the elemental tremors of desire coursing through his hard body.

"Last chance," he said thickly.

Her hips moved. Sultry fire licked over Ten. Shaking with a hunger he had never felt before, Ten knew he was going to take what he must have, what she was asking him for, what they both wanted until it was agony not to have it; but he had never taken a woman like this before, no barriers, nothing except violently sensitive skin and a need so great it kept him on the breaking edge of self-control.

When Ten's aroused flesh found the incredible softness and heat waiting for him, the sensation was so intense he couldn't breathe. He felt each separate pulse of Diana's response as he parted the soft flesh, sheathing himself within her slowly, deliberately, deeply, sharing her body and his own in an exquisite intimacy that was just short of anguish.

"I've never—been like this—before," Ten said thickly, his breath breaking. "Naked. Nothing held back. It's—I can't—"

He went utterly still, fighting desperately not to lose control.

"Tennessee," Diana whispered, looking into the silver blaze of his eyes, feeling the first waves of pleasure ravish her. "Give me your baby, Tennessee."

A sound of hunger and ecstasy was torn from Ten's throat, and then ecstasy alone, Diana's name repeated in shattered syllables as he gave himself again and again to the sweet violence of a union unlike any he had ever known.

Sixteen

Thunder cracked with a noise like rock shearing away from tall cliff faces, a naked violence of sound that made September Canyon tremble in the night.

Ten eased out of the blankets he shared with Diana and went to stand at the edge of the overhang. The chilly air took the heat from his body, but he barely noticed the temperature. The smell, taste and sound of the wind told him all that he needed to know. He and Diana would have to pack up and cross Picture Wash before dawn.

And Ten had counted on spending the hour before dawn quite differently.

"Damn."

"What's wrong?" Diana asked sleepily.

"Storm coming on. A big one."

By memory alone Ten went to the camp table, struck a match and lit the Coleman stove. The golden glow of naked flame danced in graceful reflections over the pale sandstone. He made coffee with the swift, economical motions of a man very familiar with the task. Then he walked to the warm blankets where Diana lay, grabbed his clothes and began dressing.

"Ten . . . ?"

It was only a single word, but he understood all that she wasn't saying. Reluctantly he shook his head.

"Sorry, honey," Ten said, his voice gritty with hunger and regret. "We've got a lot of packing to do and not much time to do it."

Diana bit back her protest even as it formed. The storm didn't care if it were cutting short her last hours with Ten in September Canyon.

Silently she kicked off the blankets and began pulling on clothes, shivering as the cold wind washed over her body. Working by the light of a gas lantern, she packed quickly, forcing herself not to think how this day was different from any day that had come before or would come after.

As soon as Diana's personal gear was packed, she began working on the artifacts that were to be taken back to the ranch. She packed slowly, carefully, saying goodbye with her fingertips to the ancient pots and stone axes, fiber sandals and bone implements that she had come to know as well as she knew the less textured camping equipment of her own time and culture.

When each box was ready, she set it aside for Ten to carry to the truck. Periodic lightning shattered the black sky. Thunder rang repeatedly, a barrage that deafened. She ignored it, working steadily, thinking only of the task at hand. As she reached for another empty box, she found Ten's hand instead. Startled, she looked up.

"Leave it for the grads," he said in a clipped voice. "We have to cross while we can. It's raining like hell up on September Mesa."

She looked out into the encompassing blackness and saw nothing at all. "How can you tell?"

"Listen."

At first Diana thought what she heard was the wind, a low, muttering kind of sound. Then she realized that she was hearing water. September Wash was filling.

"Is it still safe to cross?" she asked, unable to suppress the hope in her voice. If the wash weren't safe, they would be forced to stay on this side until the water went down.

As though Diana had spoken her hope aloud, Ten shook his head. "This is a big storm. Carla will fret and then Luke will send men out in hell's own rain to look for us. I don't want anyone getting hurt looking for people who could have and should have gotten back."

The sky exploded into twisting, wildly writhing forks of lightning. Barely four seconds later, thunder hammered down.

"Time to go, honey."

Diana closed her eyes against the pain that was lancing through her as surely as lightning lanced through the clouds.

Thunder filled September Canyon, followed by a gust of rain-scented wind that made piñons moan. No rain was falling, but there was no doubt that it would. Soon.

Ten opened the passenger door for Diana and helped her up into the cab. Her breast pressed against the lean male hand that was wrapped around her upper arm. Though the contact was accidental, it made every one of Diana's nerve endings shimmer. When she tried to fasten her seat belt, her hands were clumsy with the sudden rush of her blood.

Ten climbed in, saw Diana's difficulty and said, "Let me. That belt mechanism is getting kind of cranky. First you have to slack off and let it retract all the way. Like this."

He took the metal tongue from Diana's fingers, then followed the retreat of the harness across her lap. The sound of her indrawn breath was as much an inadvertent caress as his hand skimming across her body in the wake of the buckle's metal tongue. When he pulled the harness across her lap once more, his hand skimmed, hesitated for a breathless instant, then moved on. He inserted the metal tongue slowly into the locking mechanism. A subdued *click* broke the taut silence.

"See? Perfect fit." Ten's voice was low, gritty.

He touched Diana's mouth with his thumb and swore softly, wanting her. And she wanted him. It was in her eyes, in the tightness of her body, in the huskiness of the few words she had spoken. He gave her a quick, hard kiss and forced himself to concentrate on other things.

Ten drove to the wash, studied the roiling water carefully and bit off a vicious curse. There was no doubt about it, no ignoring it. The wash was definitely still safe to cross.

He put the truck in gear and drove into the water. As soon as he reached the other side he spoke without looking at Diana.

"Hang on. I'm going to drive hard to get ahead of the storm."

The road was dry and familiar, its occasional vagaries and hazards well-known to Ten. He held the big truck to a punishing pace, boring through the predawn darkness, outrunning the storm outside the truck, ignoring the one within as long as he could.

Finally the truck climbed up for the long run across Wind Mesa. For a time the road snaked along the very edge of the highland, giving a breathtaking vista of predawn light locked in luminous embrace with a high, slowly seething lid of clouds. The tenuous light was eerie, astonishing, flawless, utterly without color.

Ten stopped the truck at a point where the road gave an uninterrupted view of the dark land below.

"We're at least an hour ahead of the rain," Ten said, releasing his seat belt. "Want some coffee?"

Diana made a murmurous sound of approval that could have meant the view, the idea of coffee or both.

By the dim illumination of the dashboard lights, Ten opened a thermos and poured coffee. A clean, rich fragrance filled the cab. He handed the half-full cup to Diana, who refused it with a shake of her head.

"You first," he insisted.

"Afraid of poison?" Diana asked huskily. She forced herself to smile, concealing the sadness that had grown greater with each mile flying beneath the truck's broad tires.

Ten's own smile flashed briefly. "No, but I've discovered that coffee tastes sweeter if you drink out of my cup before I do."

Diana said his name softly, then bent her head and sipped the hot liquid. Ten flicked off the lights, killed the engine and rolled down his window. Cool air breathed across the cab, air redolent of distance and unfettered land. In silence they passed the cup of coffee between them while spectral light slowly filled the space between clouds and earth, transforming everything, infusing the very air with radiance.

"Spirit light," Ten said finally.

Diana looked up at him questioningly.

"That's what Bends-Like-the-Willow, my grandmother, called it. The kind of light that enables you to see right through to the soul of everything."

"She was Indian?" Diana asked.

Ten's smile was a thin, hard slice of white in the truck's interior twilight. "Honey, there aren't many families that were in America before the Civil War that don't have Indian blood in them. The first Blackthorns came over from Scotland more than two hundred years ago."

"Did they marry Indians?"

"Sometimes. Sometimes they just slept with them. Sometimes they fought with them. Sometimes Blackthorn women or children were taken in raids." Ten shrugged. "There has been a lot of mixing and matching of bloodlines, one way or another. If children were the result of a town marriage, they were raised white. If children were the result of no marriage, they were raised Indian."

Ten sipped coffee from the shared cup before he resumed talking about the past, because anything was better than talking about the unshed tears in Diana's eyes and the turmoil in his own mind.

"By now there's no way to tell who got which genes, native or white or everything in between. Nevada and I have black hair and a copper tone to our skin. Utah has skin like ours, but he has blond hair and black eyes." Ten shrugged. "In the end, it's the quality of the person that matters, not the rest. That's what Bends-Like-the-Willow had. Quality."

"Was it a 'town marriage'?"

He shook his head and smiled oddly. "The Blackthorns were warriors. They leaned toward informal marriages. Up until the last generation, we were raised mostly in Indian ways. Bends-Like-the-Willow was quite a woman. Her father was a MacKenzie."

"As in the Rocking M MacKenzies?"

Thunder belled again, filling the canyon.

"Probably," Ten said. "Her mother was Ute. Her father was a wild young white who rode out one night and never came back. Luke has a few like that in his family tree. One of them disappeared at about the right time and place."

"Is that how you came to own part of the Rocking M?"

Smiling sardonically, Ten shook his head. "Honey, a hundred years back, nobody gave a damn about part-Indian kids born on the wrong side of the blanket. It's only in the last generation people have started to get all puffed up and sentimental over Indian ancestors whose skeletons have been rattling in white closets for a long, long time."

"Then how did you end up here?"

"When I got out of the warrior business, I was like Nevada. Hurting and not knowing what to do about it. Needing a home and not knowing how to get one. Luke's father was selling off chunks of the Rocking M to pay for his drinking. I bought in. The ranch has been my home ever since."

Diana waited, but Ten said no more. She followed his glance out the windshield. The land lay beneath the storm

like a woman waiting for a lover. Though no rain had fallen,
the storm had brought an eerie glow to the air, a timeless
gloaming that made all distances equal. There were no
shadows to define near and far, no sun's passage to mark
hours across the sky, no waxing or waning moon to mea-
sure weeks, nothing but the eye and mind of man to draw
distinctions.

"Spirit light," Ten said, his voice harsh. "When you see
everything too damn clearly."

He looked at Diana and saw too much, his own hunger
clawing at him, telling him that he would remember her too
long, too well.

Diana looked away from the eerie clarity of the land and
saw Ten watching her with silver eyes that burned.

"What are you thinking?" she asked before she could
stop herself.

"I'm remembering."

"What?"

"How you look when your skin is flushed with heat and
you're as hungry for me as I am for you."

Knowing he shouldn't, unable to stop himself, Ten slid
partway across the big seat, took the coffee cup from Diana
and set it on the dashboard. Her dark blue glance went from
his eyes to the clean, distinct line of his mouth. Even as she
leaned toward him, he pulled her close, lifting her, turning
her so that she was half-lying across his lap. His mouth came
down over her parted lips, filling her with his taste and his
hunger, wordlessly telling her about the need that would
make the coming days restless and the nights endless.

Diana gave back the kiss without restraint, loving the taste
of Ten, coffee and man and passion. The kiss deepened even
more, becoming an urgent mating of mouths. When she felt
the hard warmth of his palms sliding beneath her sweater,
she twisted sinuously, bringing her breasts into his hands.
His fingers stroked, caressed, teased until exquisite sensations radiated from her breasts to the secret core of her,
melting her in a few shuddering moments.

With a soft whimper Diana began to move against Ten's body. She felt rather than heard the rasping groan he gave when his hands released the catch on her bra, allowing him the freedom of her breasts. He pushed up her loose sweater and bra and looked at her. Flushed by passion, soft, creamy, resilient, tipped with tight pink buds of desire, her breasts begged for his mouth.

"Baby?"

"Yes," Diana whispered huskily, raising her arms and arching her back as she reached to remove her sweater.

Ten didn't wait for her to finish. He kissed one peak, licked it with catlike delicacy, then gave in to the need driving him. His mouth opened over her in a caress that sent sensual lightning glittering through her. With a ragged cry she threw off the sweater and held his head against her breast, asking for and receiving a different, harder caress.

Even as Ten's mouth sent forerunners of ecstasy shimmering through Diana, his hands closed on her hips, shifting her until she was sitting astride his lap. One hard palm slid between her legs, cupping her, stroking her, making her burn. Sweet cries rippled from her, cries like fire consuming Ten, cries that made him wild with need. He unfastened the front of Diana's jeans and pushed his hand into the scant space between denim and her body. Hungrily he forced aside cloth until he could search through the warm nest to find the sultry woman-heat he needed to touch more than he needed air to breathe.

And then Ten found what he sought. He took as much as he could of Diana's softness and wanted more, much more, his body straining and his breath a groan.

The hoarse sound Diana made and the feel of her struggling against his hand brought Ten to his senses. He closed his eyes and took a tearing breath, afraid to look at her, afraid to see the fear and horror in her eyes as she remembered another out-of-control man, the front seat of another vehicle.

"God, baby, I'm sorry," Ten said hoarsely. "I've never lost control like that."

He heard Diana take a broken breath, then another, and felt her incredible softness pressing intimately against the hand that was still tangled in her jeans. Very carefully he dragged his hand free. Another broken sound from her scored him.

"Baby, I'm sorry," Ten whispered, looking at Diana's wide eyes, wanting to cradle her and yet afraid to touch her. "I didn't mean to frighten you."

"You—didn't."

The words were like Diana's breathing—ragged. Ten shook his head slowly, not believing her.

"I heard you," he said flatly.

"I wanted you—so much—it hurt. I didn't know—it could be like that."

The last word was spoken against Ten's lips just before he brought Diana's mouth over his own. The kiss was deep, searching, wild. She returned it with a hunger that made both of them shake.

"If you kiss me like that again," Ten said finally, breathing hard, "I'm going to start taking off those boots you're wearing."

"My boots?"

"And then your jeans," Ten said, sliding his hand inside denim once more, searching for Diana's softness, finding it, drawing liquid fire and a ripping sound of pleasure from her. "I want you. Right here. Right now. Do you want me like that?"

With fingers that trembled, Diana reached blindly for her bootlaces. Ten made a low sound as his hand slid more deeply into her jeans. He smiled almost savagely, savoring her heat and the ragged breaking of her breath. Each movement she made as she worked over her laces increased the effect of his hidden caress. Ten made no move to help with the boots, for his other hand was too busy stroking the

firm curves of her breasts to be bothered with such unre-
warding objects as boots and socks.

One boot, then the other, fell to the floor of the truck,
followed by the rustling whisper of socks. Slowly Diana
shifted her body to the side, not wanting to end the wild,
secret seduction of Ten's hand, but at the same time wanting to be free of the confinement of her jeans.

This time Ten helped, lifting Diana and peeling the rest of
her clothes away, letting them fall to the floor. She shivered
with heat rather than cold as she sat astride Ten once more.
He looked down at his lap and the woman whose body was
flushed with the passion he had aroused.

Slender hands reached for Ten's belt buckle.

"Baby, if you start there, that's where you'll finish. I want
you like hell burning."

Diana looked into the hot silver of Ten's eyes and knew
if she didn't take his boots off first, they wouldn't get taken
off at all. His hand slid up her thigh, touched, tested deeply,
knew the scalding need of her body.

"Yes," she whispered. "Like hell burning."

Watching Ten's face, Diana opened the buckle. Leather
pulled free of the loops with a sliding, whispering noise.
Metal buttons gave way in a muted rush of sound. She
reached down only to find that he was there before her, his
hard flesh parting her as he watched her take him, and he
was filling her even as she watched. Her breath unraveled
into a low moan as she was hurled into ecstasy. He drove
into her again, burying himself in the clinging, generous
heat that had haunted his dreams, and then ecstasy con-
vulsed him and he held her hard, deep inside her, his mouth
against her hot skin and her cries washing over him, echo-
ing the sweet lightning of his own release.

Locked within ecstasy, surrounded by the cruel clarity of
spirit light, Ten knew this was the way he would always remember Diana, and the realization was a knife turning,
teaching him more about pain than he wanted to know.

Seventeen

The knock on the door was both unexpected and the answer to Diana's secret hopes. Even as her heartbeat doubled, she told herself that she was being foolish.

It isn't Ten. He hasn't so much as telephoned in the weeks since I left the Rocking M, so what makes me think that he would waste a Friday driving all the way to Boulder to see me?

The cold, rational thoughts didn't diminish the fierce, hopeful beat of Diana's heart. She pushed away from her drawing table, took a deep, steadying breath and walked the few steps to her studio apartment's front door.

"Who is it?" she asked.

"Cash McQueen. Carla MacKenzie's brother."

With hands that weren't quite steady, Diana unlocked the door and opened it. Once she would have been unnerved at the sight of the big man who almost filled her doorway. Now the only emotion she felt was a disappointment so numbing that it was all she could do to speak. She forced her lips into the semblance of a smile.

"Hi. I thought you were in...South America, wasn't that it?"

"It was. I got back last week."

"Oh. Did you find what you were looking for?"

Cash smiled slowly, transforming his face from austere to handsome. His eyes lit with a rueful inner laughter. "No, but not many of us do."

Diana felt a flash of kinship with the big man. "No, not many of us do."

"May I come in?"

"Of course," she said, automatically backing away from the door, allowing Cash to enter. "Would you like some coffee? Or perhaps a beer? I think one of the grads left some here last night."

"Thanks, but I'll have coffee. Party last night?" he asked, looking around with veiled curiosity.

Diana's mouth curved in something less than a smile. "Depends on your definition of party. If it includes chasing elusive potshards through mismarked cartons, we had one hell of a party here last night."

"I thought all the September Canyon stuff was staying at the Rocking M."

"It is. This is from a different site. Still Anasazi, though, as you can see. They're my first love."

While Diana disappeared into the kitchen, Cash walked carefully around the apartment. It was in a state of casual disarray that resembled an academic office more than living quarters. Scholarly periodicals, books and photos covered most flat surfaces, except for a worktable. There, potshards and partially reconstructed pots reigned supreme. Photos and sketches were tacked to the walls. A bin full of sketches stored in protective transparent sleeves stood in a corner.

"Cream or sugar?" Diana called from the kitchen alcove.

"Black."

Cash walked over to the bin and began flipping slowly through the contents, studying various drawings. When Diana returned, he looked up.

"These are very good."

"Thank you." Diana set a mug of coffee on a table near Cash and cleared periodicals from a chair. "But photos are preferred by most scholars, unless they're trying to illustrate a point from their pet theory. Then they're delighted to have me draw what no one has yet had the good sense to discover in situ."

Male laughter filled the small room. Diana looked startled, then smiled self-consciously.

"I didn't mean that quite as peevishly as it came out," she said, clearing away a second stack of periodicals and sitting down. With a casualness that cost a great deal, she asked, "How's everything on the Rocking M?"

"That's why I'm here."

Diana's head turned quickly toward Cash. "Is something wrong?"

"You took the words right out of my mouth."

"I don't understand."

"Neither does Carla."

"Mr. McQueen," began Diana.

"Cash."

"Cash," she said distractedly. "You came here for a reason. What is it?"

With a characteristic gesture of unease, Cash jammed his hands in the back pockets of his jeans, palms out. He looked at the small woman with the haunted indigo eyes and lines of strain around her full mouth. Cash didn't know what was wrong, but he was certain that something was.

Carla, what the hell have you gotten me into this time? You know better than to try and set me up with another female in a jam.

Cash looked closely at Diana. Despite her abundant femininity, she wasn't sending out the signals that an available woman did. She had smiled at the sound of his laughter, but then, a lot of people did. They hadn't learned that laughter was a perfect camouflage for his view of people in general and women in particular. One woman, however, was exempt from Cash's distrust—Carla.

"My sister would like to see you again," Cash said, "but apparently you're angry with her."

Diana started to speak. No words came out. All she could do was shake her head.

"Does that mean Carla has it all wrong and you'd be glad to come out to the Rocking M next weekend?" Cash asked smoothly.

"No." The stark refusal was out before Diana could prevent it.

Not that it mattered. She wasn't going back to the Rocking M. Not this weekend. Not the weekend after. Not ever. She couldn't bear seeing Ten again and pretending that nothing had ever happened between them in September Canyon. Nor could she pretend that his baby wasn't growing day by day within the loving warmth of her womb.

"Carla's right," Cash said. "You're angry with her."

"No."

"With Luke?"

"No," Diana said quickly. "It's nothing personal." She licked her lips with a tongue that was dry. "I'm—I'm very busy. The school year is just getting rolling. There are a lot of things I have to do."

Cash's eyes narrowed to brilliant blue slits. "I see." And he did. He saw that Diana lied very badly. "Surely you'll have everything under control by, say, November?"

"I don't know."

"Probably?"

She gave him a dark look. "I don't know!"

"Well, I know that Carla will have a strip off my hide if you don't turn up for Thanksgiving. Now I can probably finesse my little sister, but I'd hate like hell to try finessing the Rocking M's ramrod with anything less than a bulldozer."

Color drained from Diana's face, silently telling Cash that Carla's guess had been correct: it was Tennessee Blackthorn who was keeping Diana away from the ranch.

"I can't see that the..." Diana's voice dried up. She swallowed painfully and continued. "What does Ten have to do with this?"

"You tell me."

"Nothing."

"Whatever you say," Cash muttered, not believing Diana and not bothering to disguise it. "Ten has developed a passion for all things Anasazi. If the recent past is any example, he's going to be a miserable son to live with until that kiva gets excavated."

Diana's eyelids flinched, but her voice was under control when she spoke. "Then by all means he should have the kiva excavated as soon as possible."

"Amen. How long will it take you to pack?"

"I'm not going anywhere."

"You're not making any sense, either."

"Mr. McQueen—"

"Cash."

"—the kiva can be excavated by any number of qualified archaeologists. I'm sure Ten knows it. If not, he'll know it as soon as you go back and tell him."

"I already have. He almost tore off my head. Either you excavate that kiva or it doesn't get done."

"Then it doesn't get done."

"Why?"

"Would you like more coffee before you leave?"

"None of my business, is that it?"

"That's it."

"Would it make any difference if Carla dragged the baby all the way out here to talk to you?"

"I'd love to see Carla and Logan, but they would be going home alone."

"What if Ten asked you to excavate his damned kiva?"

Diana's eyes darkened and her tone became as bittersweet as the line of her mouth. "He already did."

For the first time Cash showed surprise. "You refused?"

"Yes."

"Why?"

"Ask Ten."

"No thanks. I like my head just where it is. Lately that boy has a fuse that's permanently lit. The only one willing to take him on is Nevada. They had hell's own brawl a week ago. Never seen anything quite like it. A miracle no one was killed."

Diana remembered Nevada's dark, cold power. She closed her eyes and fought against showing her fear and love and despair. It was useless. When she opened her eyes she saw that Cash knew exactly how she felt.

"Is he all right?" Diana asked tightly.

"Nevada's a little chewed up, but otherwise fine."

"Ten," she said urgently. "Is Ten all right?"

Cash shrugged. "Same as Nevada."

Diana hesitated for a moment, then went to the bin and withdrew a two-by-three-foot folder. She opened it and silently looked at the drawing. Within the borders of the paper, September Canyon lived as it had once in the past, stone walls intact, houses and kivas filling the alcove. But the people were no longer walled off within their beautifully wrought prisons. They were responding to the call of an outlaw shaman who had seen a vision filled with light.

Women, children, warriors, every Anasazi was pouring out of the cliff dwelling, walking out of the alcove's eternal twilight and into a dawn that blazed with promise. Their path took them past the shaman, who stood in the foreground within the shadow of the cliff, watching with haunted eyes, his outstretched arm pointing the way for the stragglers as they filed past below. Something in the shaman's position, his eyes holding both light and darkness, his body removed from the other Anasazi, stated that he was not walking out of darkness with his people.

The face, the lithe and muscular body, the stance, the haunted crystalline eyes were those of Tennessee Blackthorn.

"I sketched this for the owner of September Canyon," Diana said, closing the folder and holding it out to Cash. "It's a bit awkward to mail. Would you take it to the Rocking M for me?"

"Sure." Cash looked at the folder and then at Diana. "You do know that Ten owns September Canyon, don't you?"

"Thank you for taking the sketch." Diana went to the front door and opened it. "Say hello to Carla and Luke for me."

"Should I say hello to Ten, too?" asked Cash on his way out.

Diana's only answer was silence followed by the door shutting firmly behind Cash. He raised his fist to knock on the door again but thought better of it when he heard the broken, unmistakable sounds of someone who was trying not to cry. Swearing silently about the futility of trying to talk rationally to a woman, he turned away and went toward his beat-up Jeep with long, loping strides. If he hurried, he would be at the ranch house before the afternoon thunderstorms turned the road to gumbo.

The next night, barely fifteen minutes after the last grad student left, Diana spotted the scruffy knapsack slumped in a corner. Bill usually remembered halfway home, turned around and came back. It had become a ritual—the knock on the door, the knapsack extended through the half-open door and the embarrassed apologies. Tonight, however, she wondered whether the knapsack would be an overnight resident. Bill had left with Melanie, and the look in his eyes had nothing to do with unimportant details such as knapsacks.

Diana glanced at the clock. Midnight—if Bill were going to retrieve his property, he would be back soon. With a shrug, she sat down at the table full of shards and picked up two. The edges didn't match, but that didn't matter. Diana wasn't seeing them. She was seeing other shards, other shapes and a matching that had been superb.

At least for her.

I've got to stop thinking about it. I've got to stop asking where I went wrong and why I wasn't the woman for Ten when he was the man for me. I've got to stop thinking about the past and start planning for the future. He trusted me enough to give me his baby. That has to be enough.

The sound of knuckles meeting the apartment door was a welcome break from Diana's bleak thoughts.

"Hang on. I'm coming," Diana called out.

She snagged the knapsack by its strap, opened the front door without looking, held out the knapsack at arm's length and waited for Bill to take it.

The door opened fully, pushing Diana back into the living room. The knapsack hit the floor with a soft thump, falling from her nerveless fingers.

Ten walked into the room and shut the door behind himself, watching Diana with hooded eyes that missed none of the subtle signs of stress—the brackets at the side of her mouth, the circles beneath her eyes, the body that was too thin. And most of all the eyes, too bleak, too dark.

Ten didn't know what he had expected Diana to do when he walked back into her life, but shutting down like a flower at sunset wasn't one of the things he had imagined. He kept remembering the moment when she had looked at him with eyes still dazed by pleasure and whispered that she loved him. She must have accepted his explanation that what she felt was temporary rather than lasting, for she had never mentioned love again. Yet the moment and the words had haunted him at odd moments ever since, tearing at his emotions without warning, making it painful to breathe.

But nothing had prepared him for the cruel talons sinking into him when he had opened the folder and seen himself standing alone, watching life pass by in a shimmering parade while he stood lost in shadow.

"You look tired," Diana said tonelessly. "Is the ranch still shorthanded?"

Ten made a dismissing motion. "I didn't come here to talk about the Rocking M's personnel problems."

Diana waited, asking in silence what she didn't trust herself to put into words. *Why are you here?*

"I came here to find out why you won't come back and excavate the kiva," Ten said bluntly.

"I have enough work to do in Boulder," she said, lacing her fingers together, trying to conceal their fine tremors.

"Bull."

Her hands clenched. "Why do you want me to excavate the kiva? Why not some other archaeologist?"

"You know why."

"Yes." Her lips curved down. "Sex."

Ten flinched but said nothing.

Diana turned away, knowing that she couldn't conceal her feelings any longer if she kept looking at him. When she spoke, her voice was desperately reasonable. "Don't you think that's rather a long drive just to get laid?"

Ten hissed a vicious word. "That's not what I meant and you know it!"

"Then what did you mean?"

"Are you pregnant?"

The bald question seemed to hang in the stillness like a wire being pulled tighter and tighter until it hummed just above the threshold of hearing.

"Don't worry, Tennessee," Diana said. "I keep my promises and I know you made none. Whether or not I'm pregnant, you're free."

"Dammit, Diana, *are you pregnant?*"

She let out a long, soundless breath. "You aren't listening. If I'm pregnant, I continue teaching. If I'm not pregnant, I continue teaching. Either way, I'm not going to excavate that kiva, so it makes no difference to you."

"No difference? What do you take me for!"

"A man who prefers living alone."

In the silence, the sound of Ten's sudden intake of breath was appallingly clear. Anger and the cold fear that had driven Ten since he had looked at the sketch exploded soundlessly inside him.

"You said you loved me."

More accusation than anything else, the words scored Diana. "And you told me I didn't know what love was. You told me what we had was sex. Sex doesn't last."

The bleakness of his own words coming back to him cut into Ten more deeply than any intentional insult could have. Like the sketch, the words were a wounding that sliced through old scars to the living flesh beneath.

"My God, how you must hate me," he whispered. "That's why you sketched me as an outlaw too cruel to be part of his people's freedom."

The pain beneath Ten's words shattered the last of Diana's control. She spun around, her face white. "That's not what I sketched!"

Ten's breath came in hard when he saw the tears glittering on Diana's pale cheeks. He started to speak but she was already talking, words tumbling out, her voice shaking with her need to make him understand.

"I saw a man who turned away from the possibility of love even as he freed me to love for the first time in my life, a love that you didn't believe in. But that's not the point. The point is that you gave me a great deal that is of lasting value and took as much as you wanted from me in return, and what you wanted wasn't lasting. It was a very beautiful, very passionate, very brief affair. I don't hate you. End of story."

Long, lean hands framed Diana's face. Ten bent and kissed away her tears as delicately, as thoroughly, as he had once kissed away her fear of him.

"Ten," she whispered, "don't. Please don't."

"Why? If our affair was that good," he asked in a dark velvet voice, "why can't it go on?"

"What if I—" Diana's voice broke. "Oh, Ten, don't you see? What would happen if there were a child?"

Ten bent again, taking her mouth, making it impossible for her to do anything but kiss him in return. Diana made an odd, broken sound and held on to him, taking and giving and trembling. By the time the kiss ended, she was crying wildly.

"Shh, don't cry," he said repeatedly, trying to kiss away the tears again, but there were too many this time. "Don't cry, baby. It tears me apart. I never wanted to hurt you like this. Everything is all right, baby. Don't cry."

Diana thought of the child growing inside her and felt a dizzying combination of love and despair. Ten was back, but only for a night or two. A week. Maybe even a few months.

And then he would leave again. *What we have isn't love. It passes.*

"I'm sorry—I can't stop crying and I—I can't—I can't continue our affair."

Ten made a hoarse sound that could have been Diana's name and tried without success to stem the hot silver flood with his thumbs. He kissed her gently, then kissed her again and again, breathing his words over her lips as though wanting to be certain that she absorbed his words physically as well as mentally, that she believed him all the way to her soul.

"Listen to me, Diana. You're the only woman I've ever been completely naked with." His lips brushed hers slowly. "You're the only woman I've ever trusted enough to have my child." His tongue traced her lips. "You're the only woman I've ever wanted so much it haunted me to the point that I couldn't sleep. Not just your beautiful body, but your quicksilver mind and your laughter and your quiet times and even the anger that makes your eyes almost black. I want all of you. Don't turn away from me. Please. I can't bear losing you. Tell me I haven't lost you. Tell me that you still love me."

The dark, ragged velvet of Ten's voice wrapped around Diana, stripping away her defenses, leaving only the truth of her love.

"I'll always love you," Diana said, her voice breaking. "That won't change. But other—other things will. You—I—"

Ten's mouth closed over hers in a kiss that was a promise as well as a caress, a yearning hope as well as a burning hunger, a need and a sharing as complex as love itself. When he finally lifted his mouth he was trembling with more than desire.

"I love you, Diana. It's the last damn thing in the world I expected to happen. But it did and I'm not going to fight it any longer. Don't cry, love," Ten whispered, rocking Diana against his chest. "Don't cry. Just hold on to me and let me hold on to you. I've never been in love before. I've never wanted to live with a woman, to have children with her, to build a life around something other than silence." He looked down at Diana with hungry silver eyes. "Will you marry me? Will you have my children?"

Diana tried to speak but couldn't. She took Ten's hand in hers, kissed his hard palm and silently put it over the soft curve of her body where his baby was growing. She watched his eyes widen, felt his hand probe gently, heard the sudden raggedness of his breathing.

"Diana?"

"Yes," she said, laughing and crying at once. "Oh, yes!"

Ten's arms closed around the woman he loved and he lifted her off the floor in a huge hug, laughing with a joy he had never thought to feel—an outlaw walking out of the shadowed past into a future filled with light.

* * * * *

Look for Cash McQueen's story next month in GRANITE MAN, the next book in the Western Lovers series—only in Silhouette Desire!

BEGINNING IN FEBRUARY FROM

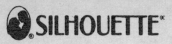

Western Lovers

An exciting new series by Elizabeth Lowell
Three fabulous love stories
Three sexy, tough, tantalizing heroes

In February, *Man of the Month* Tennessee Blackthorne in *OUTLAW*
In March, Cash McQueen in *GRANITE MAN*
In April, Nevada Blackthorne in *WARRIOR*

WESTERN LOVERS—Men as tough and untamed as the land they call home.

Only in *Silhouette Desire!*

DOU-1A

proudly presents
the long-awaited "prequel" volume of

LOVE AND GLORY
by
LINDSAY McKENNA
Dawn of Valor

In the summer of '89, Silhouette Special Edition premiered three novels celebrating America's men and women in uniform: LOVE AND GLORY, by bestselling author Lindsay McKenna. Featured were the proud Trayherns, a military family as bold and patriotic as the American flag—three siblings valiantly battling the threat of dishonor, determined to triumph . . . in love and glory.

Now, discover the roots of the Trayhern brand of courage, as parents Chase and Rachel relive their earliest heartstopping experiences of survival and indomitable love, in

Dawn of Valor, Silhouette Special Edition #649

This month, experience the thrill of LOVE AND GLORY—from the very beginning!

SILHOUETTE·INTIMATE·MOMENTS®

NORA ROBERTS
Night Shadow

People all over the city of Urbana were asking, Who was that masked man?

Assistant district attorney Deborah O'Roarke was the first to learn his secret identity . . . and her life would never be the same.

The stories of the lives and loves of the O'Roarke sisters began in January 1991 with NIGHT SHIFT, Silhouette Intimate Moments #365. And if you want to know more about Deborah and the man behind the mask, look for NIGHT SHADOW, Silhouette Intimate Moments #373, available in March at your favorite retail outlet.

NITE-1

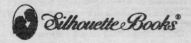

Silhouette Books®

Take 4 bestselling love stories FREE

Plus get a FREE surprise gift!